GREENROCK ROAD

JENNIFER WALTERS

BARBRA JUNE PUBLISHING

For my grandmother, Irene Hardy
Truly the most beautiful person I know.
Thank you for making my childhood so memorable.
You were always my person.
Xo

FEBRUARY

CHAPTER 1

Emily

*D*espite the freezing cold in Minnesota, Hibbing was a good place for Emily Fredrickson to forget her past and keep her secrets hidden.

Of course, some of her life was no longer secret, like Matthew and his drug abuse. She was embarrassed at not realizing Matthew was using again until it was too late. Looking back, the signs were there, but she refused to see them. When they met, she was sure their love was meant to be. She ran into him at the gas station, literally. She ended up in the emergency room with an injured leg, and he was by her side. His license had been sent to him, but instead of his picture, it had hers but with his information on it. What were the odds? One crazy mix up. She was sure fate brought them together.

"I don't want to scare you off, but I do have a drug problem I've been struggling with for so long."

His eyes were so sad as if they were begging her to help him.

"You need to get help," she said. She knew she should run away, but there was something about him sitting there and begging her for help she just could not turn his back to him.

"If I get help, will you be here when I get out?"

The question caught her off guard. She just met him. He just met her. Was this not weird that he was asking her to wait for him? He leaned in and kissed her. His lips touched hers and her body felt warm all over. "I'll wait for you," she said.

At the time she thought it was romantic. They were brought together so she could save his life and be his hero. It worked, for a while anyway. She loved counting down the days until he got out of rehab. He called and asked if she would visit but she said no. He needed this time to get better. "I don't want you to relapse because of me. I'm not going anywhere, Matthew. I'm here to fight with you."

"You're right," he said. "You are my angel."

It wasn't long after he got out of rehab he asked her to be his wife. He took his sobriety seriously and she fell hard and fast. His family treated her like she had been around forever. She thought his use was far behind him. They were living happily ever after, or so she thought. Matthew started drinking and doing drugs, which cost him his job working at the prison. He hid his emotions by drinking when she told him she was pregnant.

"I'm going to be a father," he said, calling pretty much everyone they knew. She thought it was too soon for him to be telling everyone, but she did not say anything. He was so happy, or so she thought.

He thought his life was falling apart and he was scared, so he did the only thing he knew to do. He turned to meth to forget his problems. She was so tired she passed out when her head hit the pillow at night. He was never around and she took care of Irene on her own. She liked it better that way because for some reason she just did not trust him anymore. She seldom knew whether or not Matthew came to bed at night. Nor did she notice how thin he had become, that his eyes were sunken, and the late-night phone calls and deliveries. She was ashamed for not caring enough to see that her husband was an addict. What kind of wife never noticed her husband was using and selling meth? She had promised she would be there for him but she failed him.

Irene's third birthday was held at the planetarium. They invited fifteen little kids and their parents to watch *Frozen* on the big screen. Matthew showed up but she avoided him. He had just come home from working midnights at the prison. He was likely crabby from lack of sleep so she kept her distance from him at the party.

"Mommy, can I have some more popcorn?"

"Sure honey, just give me a minute."

She opened the door to the concession stand. Matthew was on the floor, elbows on the carpet, butt in the air. His sister, Gabby, was inches down there beside him, her face contorted. She pulled on his arms and shoulders. "Get up, now!"

Tears rolled down Matthew's face. "You don't understand. I need to find them. I can't live without them. They're coming to get me, and they'll kill me if I don't have them. Help me!"

Gabby pulled him up by the arm like a small child.

He shrieked, cried, and screamed as he punched Gabby in the face. "It's mine! You can't have it!"

Gabby's eye swelled up and was turning black.

"Call 911, Emily! He's high and out of control."

Gabby must be wrong Matthew did not use anymore.

Gabby must have misinterpreted the situation. He was at his child's birthday party. He was not high.

Matthew turned and looked at her. His head was twitching, his eyes were red, and he was so thin. How many days had he been wearing those same clothes? The pock marks on his face? The bags under his eyes? And what was that smell? When was the last time he slept, and when did she lose track of her husband? When did he start sleeping on the couch because he could not fall asleep in bed beside her? When was the last time he sat down to eat with her? When was the last time they had sex, cuddled, or had a conversation? Was Gabby right? Was he using?

She held his face in her hands. "Are you doing meth again?"

She stared deep into his ocean blue eyes as if the answers were hidden in there. But his eyes were blank.

He jumped back and screamed at her.

Everyone at the birthday party had moved into the front entrance of the planetarium and clasped their children close as they stared at the hobo who they all thought was her husband.

She shaded her eyes with her hand and looked away.

Matthew ran for the door. A young police officer tackled him. He was tall and scrawny, but he had about forty pounds on her skeletal husband.

She was not sure when everyone from the party left, or what Matthew said to her. Gabby later told her he thought someone was coming to kill him, and he was searching for the crystals he swore he dropped on the floor. Matthew told the police someone had set him up, and he had proof because they were following him and broke into his house the previous night. That was not true. He was working midnights at the prison.

Irene's birthday would forever be remembered as the day

the town of Hibbing watched Irene's father get arrested for meth.

Wherever she went, she was met with forced nods from acquaintances. People turned away from her and Irene as they shopped for groceries or attended the public library for story time. They seemed to think she had a part in it, and maybe they were right. How did she not see this coming? How could she not have known? This was what everyone was thinking, and it was what she was thinking.

Gabby tried to help. "They feel bad for you, hon. They don't know what to say."

She shook her head. "No one feels bad for me, please they are disgusted with me ."

In a small town like Hibbing, reputation was everything, and she had worked hard to push down her past and come out of her shell. Hibbing was not a place where the neighbors brought over a fresh apple pie or lasagna to welcome new people into their neighborhood. Not right away, anyway. A newcomer needed to gain their trust first, and that was true even at her job. Once a person lived in Hibbing long enough to be considered a resident, the neighbors bent over backward for each other. Except now their eyes were full of judgment and some were not quiet about their thoughts when she and her daughter walked by.

SHE STARTED her car and it turned over slowly, coughing and sputtering, squealing like it was desperately struggling for air in the grip of mother nature's icy cold hands. "I love you, Hooptie, come on baby, I need you right now." She rubbed the cold steering wheel and smiled when it responded. The Iron Range made up a small portion of northern Minnesota mining towns, and Hibbing was about an hour North of Duluth.

. . .

SHE RAN straight from her car into the warm office, almost hitting her boss, Mr. Rivers, in the back with the door. "Oh, I'm sorry, Mr. Rivers ..."

The words died at the frown on his face, which was anything but welcoming. His Oxford pink button-down dress shirt was wrinkly and had a dark stain the size of a quarter near his belly button, which made it hard for her to stop staring. Mr. Rivers was always complaining about everything. He was a type A, always had to be right and never listened to ideas from any of his staff. He hid behind his office doors and only talked with customers over the phone. He never had the staff's backs with complaining customers.

She had worked for him for close to four years now. Her success was a big reason for the growth in the company, and Mr. Rivers replacing the fifties distressed oak desks with brand new cherry oak desks and Apple computers. Never once did he give her a pat on the back and he always questioned her decisions. He was hard on her, but he seemed to speak highly of her to her co-workers, which made no sense to her.

"EMILY, would you come into my office?"

Something was wrong. Was he upset because she almost hit him with the door? How was she supposed to know he would be standing in front of it like an idiot.

He straightened his tie and cleared his throat. "It's a cold one today, isn't it?"

"Yep." Get to the point. He may not understand the concept of hard work, but she had a lot to do this morning including a dozen calls to make before ten.

She chewed on her lip. "What's this all about, Mr. Rivers?

I know you didn't call me in here to say good morning or talk about the weather."

He reddened. "Okay, okay, you've always had great instincts."

Sweat beads were collecting on his forehead. "I'll cut to the chase. You've done a great job here, and your work is impeccable. We both know this company has been struggling for quite some time ..."

Her stomach churned. He would not dare. Would he?

"But the time has come, and I'm going to have to let you go."

She stood up, a fire burning in the pit of her stomach." You and I both know I've put my heart and soul into helping this company grow into what it's become. This is because of my husband, isn't it?"

He shifted in his chair, and straightened his tie once again. "No, it isn't just about him and what happened--"

"Look me in the eye and tell me it isn't about Matthew. You can't fire me for what my husband did, I can sue you."

Mr. Rivers cleared his throat and brought her back to the present. His cheeks flushed at her comment. "Emily, I'll be honest with you, our clients are shying away. You know how judgmental people are in this small town. We're hurting as it is. They mean well and with time it will pass, but I can't afford to keep you on any longer."

"Don't do this, please. I'll call and talk to each and every one of them, I promise!" She could not lose her job it was all she had left. How would she pay her bills? Could he get away with this? Could he even run this company without her? She doubted it.

"I'm sorry."

He walked over to her, and a look of pity crossed his face. He tried to put his hand on her shoulder, but she pushed it away.

"I can't deal with this right now, I can't. You know how good I am. Just last year I had the top sales in the company and the most referrals. Trust me, I'll be back on top in no time." Was she trying to convince him or herself?

Mr. Rivers took a step back. "If there was anything I could do, I'd do it. You know that. The threats keep coming in from clients. It's you or their business and I'm sorry, I just can't take that chance."

"You know what? Fine, I quit." Could she quit when she had already been fired? She did not care because it felt good.

She slammed his office door and made her way down the hall.

Her eyes were blurry, but she would not cry, not here, not now. No one would get the satisfaction of seeing her break down.

She packed up her stuff in the box already on her desk. How thoughtful of him. She grabbed the wedding picture of her and Matthew and threw it into the garbage. The glass cracked in half. She let out a grunt, finished packing up the rest of her stuff, and then stared at the picture lying in the refuse. She opened the back of the broken frame and pulled the picture out of the glass and placed it in the box.

"Damn you, Matthew."

CHAPTER 2

*J*illian was doing a jigsaw puzzle on the living room table when she walked in. Her face fell when she saw the tears in Emily's eyes. Jillian tucked her beneath her chin and wrapped her arms around her. "Oh honey, is this about Matthew? Are you okay?"

She forced a smile. "I can't live in Matthew's house any longer."

"Oh dear, don't feel that way. Did he tell you to get out? That's your house, too." Jillian was very disappointed in Matthew's choices and made sure to let Emily know every time she saw her. Emily knew her intentions were pure and that she loved Matthew, but she did not want to see Emily with him when he was acting this way. She was Matthew's aunt and she helped raise him, but she knew what was best for both Emily and Irene was to let him go so Emily could move on with her life. Be happy.

"He won't call me back or answer my letters. How didn't I know? Am I a horrible wife? Person?"

Jillian handed her a tissue off the counter. "You look at

me. You have been like a daughter to me. I love Matthew, but you don't deserve this. You need to let him go."

"I can't. I love him."

"I know, dear. Matthew loves you and Irene, but he's just so lost. You're passionate and caring and an amazing mom. You've given him more chances than you should have, but you need to give it some time. He's pulling you down, and I hate to say it, but letting him go may be the best thing for the both of you." Jillian told her this so many times already.

Old memories surfaced. She fell in love with Matthew the moment she looked into his eyes that fateful day at the gas station. He wore the same lost and broken look her mother had for years. He needed her. She remembered his black eyes and weak body, but she saw through it all and straight into his heart. He was broken and needed someone to lead the way for him. To believe in him.

"I was fired from my job today."

"You're kidding, why?"

"You know why. Matthew."

Jillian's mouth dropped open, and she stared at Emily as if the explanation was there somewhere on her face. "I'm sorry, I can't believe Mr. Rivers would sink so low."

She shook her head. "It's all about numbers."

Jillian took her hand and placed a key in it. "Emily, go up to the family cabin in Side Lake and get out of that house of yours. It can't be healthy living there after everything that's happened. Lake life is so relaxing, especially when it gets warmer and you can enjoy the water. The cabin may be a little dusty, but my neighbor has been checking on the place regularly, and it should be pretty warm. Take all the time you need. I'll be retiring up there come next year, but for now it's yours."

Should she say yes to this generous offer? This was Matthew's family cabin. She knew Destiny would want her to go and make new memories with her granddaughter, but a part of her felt guilty. The family cabin was just twenty minutes north of Hibbing on a beautiful chain of five lakes connected by short channels. One lake had a restaurant and a beautiful resort.

"I couldn't, Jillian, I just couldn't."

"Why not?"

"For one thing, I can't afford the amount you pay in lakeshore taxes."

"Emily, money is one thing I don't have an issue with. If you are there, I don't have to worry about anyone breaking in. You'd be doing me a favor. Let me keep Irene for a few days while you clean out all the dust and spiders. Please do this for me, for Irene? She would just love it there."

She needed to get away from the house that held so many reminders of her marriage. She hated Matthew for what he had done even though he could not help himself. She was sick of the daily judgment from everyone in this town, and she could only imagine how Matthew felt barred up in a prison. She could move to Side Lake, apply for jobs, and take some time for her, away from all the sadness. "Are you sure?" She knew she could not turn down this invitation.

"Yes, I'm sure. Just wait until summer, you're going to love it there. Sidelakers are much different than Hibbing people. You'll see."

ONLY A FEW CARS were on the road due to the freezing cold temperatures, but someone was catching up to her on rural highway five. She glanced at her speedometer, fifty miles per hour with these wind gusts was not bad, so how fast was this guy going? His lights blinded her from behind, and she saw an outline of a pickup truck when he turned on his blinker and began to pass her, but the headlights from another car came toward them at the same time. She tried to slow down her car, to let the truck get ahead of her, but it was too late. The truck swerved in front of her, hit her car, and sent her car flying toward the ditch.

She white-knuckled the steering wheel and pressed on the breaks, but her car hit a patch of ice and turned into a 360-degree spin. Snow crashed over the windshield like a tidal wave burying a boat when she hit the ditch. Her body shot forward, and her seatbelt pulled against her chest and her face slammed against her airbag like she had hit a brick wall. She fought to control her breathing. She only had a few minutes before she froze to death in this cold. All she could think about was if she would ever get out of this car.

A spotlight shone through her back window. Had the truck come back? Why was the truck in such a rush to pass her right before the corner? She put her key in the ignition and tried to start the car. Nothing. "Come on, Hooptie. Start."

She tried the door handle, but before she touched it, it opened. A man peeked his head in the door, then stepped out of the way so she could get out. "Are you okay?" he said.

She tried to get out, but she was trapped and her body would not move.

"Try unfastening the seatbelt," he said.

She knew that voice.

"Do you need help? You know you can't drive out of here, right? You're buried in a mountain of snow."

He reached out his hand, and she pushed it away. "I'm fine." She looked into his eyes. Her instincts were right. It was definitely him.

"It's buried deep in the snow and this ditch is steep. I don't see you coming out of here any time soon. Let me see if I can reverse it at all," he said.

The snow was mainly on the hood of her car. She had plenty of space next to her door, but her passenger door was snowed in.

The lights from his vehicle blinded her, and she barely made out his face. "How dare you try to pass me with a corner up ahead. What are you? An idiot? You could have killed me."

"It wasn't me."

"What do you mean, it wasn't you? You tried to pass me in your stupid truck and you almost killed us both."

"But it wasn't me," he said. "Look, it's too cold to argue out here. Why don't you get in my car and warm up. I'll see if I can get your car out of the ditch. You can yell at me more when I'm done."

She let out a groan. Her face burned from the cold, and her fingers were freezing inside the sleeves of her jacket. "Fine, but you're paying for the tow truck, this is your fault."

The cop light on the side mirror of his truck was still shining in her face. The lip of the ditch was higher than she thought as she crawled her way up the steep incline to his car. He did not have a hope of reversing up this hill.

She got into his car and crossed her arms. Then it struck her. She was in a car. The person who passed her drove a truck. This man was not the guy who tried to pass her. She groaned again. She had made a complete fool of herself and treated him terribly. And she knew him. Did he recognize her? Why was he living way up North? She could understand if he was living in Duluth or back in Ft. Myers, but Hibbing? Old memories flooded her, and her heart beat faster. This was the last thing she needed to deal with today.

He got out of her car and brushed off her hood with a window scraper. He opened the hood, tinkered a few minutes, then slammed it shut and scrambled up the ditch.

His black jacket and matching stocking cap made him

disappear into the night, only to suddenly appear at the driver side door. She jumped.

"Well, it's not starting, and it wouldn't matter if it did. The damage looks minimal, but it is hard to really tell until daylight. We'll have to call a tow. Where can I take you? I'm sure they won't be able to get to it tonight in this weather."

She stared into his familiar eyes and turned her head away. It was him. "Would it be an inconvenience to take me up to my cabin on Greenrock Road?"

She'd rather go with anyone but him, but she had no other options if she wanted to get to the cabin before she froze to death waiting for help to arrive. She hated that she was letting him know where she lived, but she had no choice.

"Not a problem."

"I just have to get a few things out of my trunk."

She trudged through the snow and down into the ditch. He followed her, and helped transfer all of her stuff into his trunk. By the time they finished her fingers were numb.

"Where were you going in this weather?" she said.

"I was on my way to Hibbing, but it's too damn cold to go to town anyway."

She rubbed her hands together to warm them up. "If the truck wasn't yours, how did you see what happened?"

He glanced at her and laughed. "I was driving the car that truck almost collided with. I wanted to be a kind citizen and stop to make sure you were alright, but you yelled at me."

"Oh, sorry about that. I was just so upset and then my car and--"

"It's fine. I'm just giving you some crap and trying to make you feel bad. Did it work?"

"Yes, actually. I am sorry I was rude and ignorant, and I owe you an apology.. Thank you for the ride."

"You're welcome. Where do you live up here?"

Did he really not recognize her at all? "Greenrock Road,

but I haven't been here in quite a while so I'm not sure where the turn is. Should I turn on my GPS?"

He laughed. "No, I know where Greenrock Road is, I live on it as well."

"Oh." She pulled her scarf higher on her face to conceal her identity. She had spent too many years hiding her secrets to be caught now.

He smiled and something in his eyes made her think he had an idea who she was. Who was she kidding? He used to know her so well. He continued to follow the road almost as if he was hard in thought. Luckily the driveway had been plowed or his car would not have made it through the snow and to the cabin.

"You never gave me your name," he said. "You sound so much like an old friend of mine."

She pretended not to hear. "Take a right up here, it's this one. Can you open up the trunk, please?"

He helped carry her things and followed her inside the cabin. She turned on the lights. The cabin was chilly, but the power was on.

"Is there anything I can help you with before I leave?"

She stared into those beautiful brown eyes, feeling hypnotized and angry. She forced herself to look away.

"Emily? Emily, is that you? I can't believe it. How are you?"

Her eyes widened and her knees gave out beneath her. "I think you should go, thanks for your help."

He took off his stocking cap to see her better, or maybe it was so she could see him better. "It's me, Dawson," he said, stepping in front of her.

He still had that curly, dark hair, untamed on his sweaty head. She smiled awkwardly. "Hi. What a small world, I guess."

She tried to play it off like the last time she saw him no

longer hurt, but it was hard. Her blood was boiling.

He moved closer to her until he was only a couple feet away. "I can't believe it's you. It's been far too long. Over a decade, I'd say. "

Seeing him, being this close to him, was so hard. "Yep, long time. Listen, I'm sorry to cut this short, but I am exhausted and really need to get to bed."

She turned away from him.

He walked over to the wall, turned the furnace dial, and made his way to the door. "I take it you're still angry with me about what happened. Please let me explain. Could we maybe have some coffee tomorrow, catch up?"

"I'm married," she said. The words came rolling off her tongue without thinking. "It was great to see you though."

He stepped back, his perfect brow wrinkled in thought. "Congratulations on getting married. Please think about my offer, it's just coffee. You know me, Em, I'm really sorry, and I want to make it up to you. Give me a chance to explain, please?"

"There's nothing to talk about, really. It's all good and that was a long time ago."

"Jordan was my cousin," he said. "You have to understand, I had no choice."

Just hearing his name after all these years increased her anxiety, and memories she never wanted to experience again rose to the surface. "Dawson, please just stop. I don't want to hear it." Her voice cracked.

"I'm sorry," he said, but he moved closer.

Her face burned red hot and she stepped back. But he moved closer and placed his hand on her shoulder. An intimate gesture that covered her arms in goose bumps at his touch.

"It's so great to see you. I really missed you," he whispered, just inches from her ear. "I screwed up and I know that now. I was young and dumb."

She shivered. Their eyes locked. He reached out his hand and slowly took off her hat. She went weak in the knees at his touch. He ran his fingers down the side of her face, and her eyes closed in response.

"Please have coffee with me, Em," he said softly. "I'll leave my card in case you change your mind. I have a feeling we'll be seeing a lot of each other." He set the card down on the table.

He turned around without another word and walked out the door as he put his hat back on his head. He left her aching for his touch. She dared not get too close or her secrets might come out.

She locked the door behind him and stood with her back against it, her hand still on the door handle. She closed her eyes and listened for his car to leave. Nothing. She peeked out the window. He had parked to the far right of her drive-way, where their driveways combined, and he was walking into the three-story house next door.

HER HEART STOPPED BEATING as she watched him take off his jacket through the big bay window facing her cabin. He grabbed a water bottle out of his fridge. When he took off his shirt and started unbuttoning his pants, she dropped the curtain and turned around.

She sat down at the table and woke up her cell phone. "Gabby, I'm so glad you answered. You will never believe the day I've had."

CHAPTER 3

The cute cabin had three bedrooms, a shower, a good-sized kitchen, living room, and dining room. Perfect for her and Irene. A large front window looked to the south with a view of Dawson's home. A stacked washer and drier were off the kitchen, and the front entry way had a little screen porch connected to the house. Rustic ruby red carpet covered the living room floor.

She cleaned the spider webs and dust while talking on the phone to Gabby. She did not want insects climbing into her mouth or over her face while she was sleeping. Most of the webs and two sneaky spiders hung from the window and the ceiling. She wiped them away with the broom. The rest could wait until the morning.

"It needs a little TLC, but I really like it."

"You like it because you are finally away from my brother. You know I love him, but you need to move on. Your old flame living next door sounds like a sign to me," Gabby said.

"We never even dated technically, and you know I still love your brother."

Gabby sighed.

"The dust is unbelievable. I just can't believe we never used this place," Emily said, wiping off the last window in the cabin. Four sneezes in a row and that was enough cleaning for the night. "Goodnight Gabby. I've got to get some sleep. I'll call you in the morning. Thanks for listening to me."

She turned off the lights, still in her clothes, and lay down on top of the bedspread. The heat was taking forever to warm the house to a more comfortable temperature, but she'd rather be cold then get under the sheets with dust and creepy crawlers. She pulled the afghan off the couch and snuggled under it, not bothering to even take off her boots.

She fell asleep curled in a fetal position, hungry and cold, and trying not to think about Dawson and all he used to mean to her, before all the deception and secrets.

Dreams of critters crawling on her skin woke her several times in the night. She had a lot of work ahead of her.

.

She also dreamed of Dawson that night, and flashbacked to their childhood together.

The hot sun was blinding her as she climbed on the diving board.

"Emily, if you look straight ahead you can see the ocean from there."

She looked out to see the waves crashing onto the shore. Dawson was not lying when he said the view from his diving board was the most beautiful view he had ever seen, even if he was just saying that to help her to overcome her fears.

Her knees and ankles were shaking uncontrollably. She took a deep breath and felt for the end of the diving board with her toes. She looked at him and smiled as she bent her knees to make the diving board wiggle.

"You're doing it! I knew you could do it."

She laughed and covered her face as she screamed, "Okay, here I go."

"Emily, what in the hell do you think you are doing? Get off of there!"

Startled, she slipped and hit her head on the diving board.

The next thing she knew, she was waking up in the ER. Dawson's hand was in hers. His worried eyes brightened when she looked at him.

"You're awake! Oh Em, I'm so sorry."

Her mother was dozing in a chair, which meant she was probably passed out. Her mother was the one who had screamed and over-reacted as usual, causing her to end up with a concussion. She had a life jacket on, and Dawson's mom was lying on the lawn chair watching them. There was no reason for her mom to freak out like that.

When their eyes met, her troubles faded and Dawson's whole face lit up. "Are you okay? I'm so sorry. I thought over-coming your fear—oh I don't know what I thought. I'm so sorry."

She had a hard time talking because her head hurt so much when she moved. His rambling was adorable. She wanted to reach out and lift up his chin. Tell him it was not his fault, but it hurt too much to move.

She began vomiting profusely. Dawson grabbed the tray and held it under her chin, his other hand holding her hair back. It was probably the most embarrassing moment of her life, but he did not seem disgusted at all.

"Would you like me to wake up your mom? She's been so worried about you," Dawson said.

She shook her head but had to stop and squeeze her eyes shut at the pain.

"It's okay, I won't wake her. I was so scared I was going to lose you. Emily, I would never want anything to happen to you, you're my best friend. I really hope you know that."

Those words made the pain go away for a moment. She smiled at him. He had never held her hand before, but she wanted to hold his for the rest of her life, even if she was only ten at the time. Dawson did not care that she lived in a trailer park down the street. He insisted it was more of a home than his own house.

She woke up from her dream, smiling at the past they had shared. Growing up without much money in Fort Myers was not easy, but Dawson never seemed to care. He complimented her second-hand clothes, and he told her it was just a place to live and that happiness was something much deeper than money. To him, she was the kindest person because she was not born wealthy like he was, and she made him a better person. Was he telling the truth or trying to make her feel better?

Everything changed between them the day they went swimming in the ocean with Dawson's parents. Her sister, Jamie, had just turned twenty and moved to San Francisco to live with her boyfriend that morning so she was feeling a little down. Dawson talked her into going to the beach because he always said, "There is nothing the warm sun and cold ocean water couldn't fix." Her mother had insisted her sister, Lindsey, go with them or Emily could not go. Lindsey was a year younger than her, but much prettier and developed compared to her stick figure and flat chest at the time.

Dawson and Lindsey built sand castles while she hid under an umbrella with every inch of her body covered in sunscreen and a white t-shirt. She had burned the day before and had blisters on her shoulders. The doctor told her she could not be in direct sunlight so her father insisted on an umbrella if she was going to the beach. It was non-negotiable. Just a second in the sun was enough to convince her to obey his wishes. Hot sun shining on a sunburn was torture.

Dawson and Lindsey raced to finish their castles within

two hours because Emily was supposed to be timing them. Building sandcastles was something Emily and Dawson always did together, racing to beat the stopwatch. She was angry and jealous at how much fun they were having. She tried to read her book but she could not help staring at them. Dawson was her best friend, and one day she would marry him. One day he would see her as more than just a friend.

They finished building their sand castles. "Hey Jordan, pick the winner," Dawson called to his cousin. Jordan had just moved to town from Minnesota. He was good looking, but Emily only had eyes for Dawson. She knew Jordan came from a broken home and was staying with Dawson's family. Dawson said all Jordan wanted was to move back to Minnesota and he was sick of hearing him complain about it. After all, they were in the sunshine state.

Jordan joined them. "Lindsey's castle is the best," he said without hesitation or even looking at them. Clearly Dawson's was way better and everyone knew it.

Dawson jumped on her castle and the whole thing came crashing down.

Emily smiled.

"Hey! That wasn't nice."

Lindsey chased him through the sand.

"You jerk," she said, trying and failing to catch him.

As Lindsey chased Dawson into the ocean, Dawson's cousin sat down next to her. "You think you're too good for castle building?"

Emily crossed her arms and pulled up her sleeves to show him the water blisters beneath her skin. She popped one, but it burned so much she did not touch them again. She now believed the doctor that the blisters were there to heal her skin.

He looked at her shoulders and winced. "Yikes, no

wonder you're under an umbrella, but you do know umbrella's kill people, right?"

She shook her head and played along. "They're real serial killers, aren't they?"

Dawson threw Lindsey into the waves. Emily rolled her eyes.

"I'm serious. They fly away and kill people on the beach. It happens all the time. I saw it on 20/20."

She was not impressed, nor did she care to think about it.

"You're really beautiful, you know that?"

She smiled and threw a handful of sand at him. She had difficulty taking a compliment, but she wanted Dawson to notice Jordan was flirting with her. Maybe he would be jealous, too.

"What? I'm serious. How about you and I take off and get something to eat? It has to be torture having to hide under this umbrella and watch everyone else have a good time."

Dawson and Lindsey were still laughing and flirting. She needed to leave, she had seen enough. "That sounds like a great idea."

Jordan was charming and cute, and the more time she spent with him, the more he grew on her. She had a fight with Dawson after the beach incident. She yelled at him for flirting with Lindsey and he denied it, saying he was just having fun. She did not believe a word of it, but her crush on Dawson was just that, a crush. As she and Jordan became more serious, she spent less time with Dawson. She was pretty sure he was seeing Lindsey for a little while, but they never admitted it to her. They both just happened to disappear at the same time.

Her relationship with Jordan was different than it was with her and Dawson. He was more troubled and she needed to comfort him, whereas with Dawson, he always knew the right things to say to make her feel better.

Jordan moved fast sexually, and she finally gave in because it was easier. The first time was not romantic like she thought it would be. She lost her virginity on the beach with sand in every crease in her body. The sex was nothing like in the movies, sexy and wonderful and passionate. Instead, it left her feeling insecure and depressed.

For Jordan it was all about sex, but she could not get into it. She loved him, but when he wanted it, he wanted it now. She said yes when he asked because she got sick of hearing him complain. "If you loved me I wouldn't have to convince you," he would say.

HER MOTHER'S health continued to decline. She was forgetful, mean, and she slept all the time. The day after Emily graduated from high school, she found her mom passed out on the floor, not breathing. She called 9-1-1, did CPR, but the hospital said it was too late. Her mother was dead.

Jordan was not a fan of funerals, so Dawson stood by her side as she screamed and cried and put herself back together with his help. Jordan claimed he wasn't feeling well, and he couldn't make it to the funeral, but in truth death scared him and he was uncomfortable talking about it.

Her dad was on some heavy sedatives, which left him in a zombie state. Lindsey made dinner and kept an eye on him. It was the only thing that helped her through it, staying busy.

Emily sat up all night with Dawson the night of her mother's funeral. They told stories about their childhood and they laughed and cried together. They ate junk food and danced to Puff Daddy and Tupac. They jumped on her bed until her father came up and yelled at them. She cried and Dawson rubbed her head in his lap and told her how sorry he was. Then she would laugh and dance around with red blotches on her face and a stuffed-up nose from all the crying. He started a pillow fight with her goose feathered pillows, which ended up all over the bedroom. Once one broke open, he threw the feathers in the air so they came down all around her head. She loved it. She broke open another pillow on purpose and did the same. It was so good not to care about getting in trouble. It was the least of her worries.

At five in the morning they finally went to sleep. She lay on the bed, and he wrapped his arms around her. She turned her body toward his, and their faces were just a breath away. They stared into each other's eyes for a long time. She remembered the sweetness of his breath. He always had a lemon drop in his mouth, and she loved the sourness of the scent.

"Do you ever wonder what heaven is like?" she said.

He smiled as he stared at the sun rising outside the window. It was as though the sun was rising just for them at this moment.

"All the time."

"Did you ever wonder what it would be like if we kissed?"

He looked into her eyes without saying a word. She wanted to know before it was too late. She leaned in and their lips locked. She expected him to pull away or tell her no, but he kissed her back. The taste of his mouth was like that lemon drop, sweet and passionate, and so unlike the kisses she shared with Jordan. She wanted to rip his clothes off, she wanted the moment to last forever.

He kissed her on the forehead and pulled her into his chest. "I will always love you, Emily."

They slept unit noon when Jordan came in and found them spooning. That was the day he convinced her to move to Minnesota with him. He claimed he wanted to get away from the heat, but he really wanted to get her away from Dawson. She agreed, wanting to escape the place where she was known as the girl who found her dead mother. She needed to start all over. Anywhere was better than here, where she was haunted with horrible memories.

She told Jordan nothing happened with Dawson, and he blew her off. "Dawson is my cousin. He would never do that to me. I was never worried about him."

They said their goodbyes, and Dawson met them at their car when it was all packed up. As he pulled her in for a quick hug, she closed her eyes and held back the tears. Was she making the right move?

"Don't be a stranger," Jordan said to Dawson.

His body became smaller and smaller in the side mirror of their car as they drove away. Jordan reached over and squeezed her hand. She had felt nothing in return.

SHE LAY in bed with all the memories circling in her head. Would the guilt and anger every go away?

CHAPTER 4

*E*mily began applying for jobs first thing in the morning. She applied for a pupil support assistant position working with children at the local school, and she applied for a position as a library aid. The pay was not bad and she would get benefits if she got the PSA job. Helping to take care of children was what she loved to do most.

She ran her finger over the card, Kersich & Myer Carpentry, that Dawson had left behind in case she changed her mind about having coffee with him.

Matthew and his family knew she had issues with her family back in Florida, but she never told them the true secrets of her past. She was ashamed, but by keeping the secrets inside maybe they would go away. She worried for years she would run into Jordan. Hopefully he moved far away. She never wanted to see him again.

The cabin was warming up to her standards, and she took off her boots. The cozy cabin was exactly what she needed, but thankfully, Irene was not there to see all the dust and spider webs. She had a long way to go to get the cabin cleaned, but it looked nowhere near as bad as it did the night before. Destiny, Matthew's mother, who had passed away a few years ago, would have been angry to see the cabin so unkept. She and Matthew's father bought it together, and it was left to Matthew's aunt, Jillian, after they both passed.

She was close to Matthew's mom before she died. It all happened so fast, leaving the whole family in shock. They were glad she did not suffer, but Destiny was the glue that held the family together. Destiny had confided in Emily that she had a mother who died of drug abuse, too. Destiny would have wanted her to help Matthew until he got better again. She had thanked her so many times for saving him from his addiction. "If it wasn't for you, my son would be dead in a gutter somewhere or in prison," Destiny had told her.

GABBY CALLED. "Please come visit me for the weekend. Travis is in Minneapolis so it is just me and the kids here."

She had a hard time saying no to Gabby. She was her best friend. Gabby was so understanding through all of Matthew's crises. She was his sister, but after everything Matthew put her through, Gabby urged her to stay away from him. They put on a fundraiser together every year, raising money for children in the foster care system, although this year it was going to have to be pushed back to sometime in the winter. She could not hold up her end of the work, not with everything going on.

"Why don't you come to the cabin? Jillian can hang out with the kids, and we can paint and clean. I've got wine and pizza."

Gabby was silent. "I don't know, Em. I mean I love spending time there, but it makes me think of Phillip and the friendship we lost when we started dating. It's just so hard because it makes me think about my dad, too."

"Come on, I'm going to be staying here for quite a while

and summer is coming. If you don't start getting used to it, I'm going to end up spending the whole summer alone up here."

"You're right, I'll come."

"Really?"

"Really."

At least she would have some company. She missed Matthew and worried about him even though he was in a minimum-security prison. Was the food okay, and did he sleep at night? He refused to talk to her. Not so long ago he worked at a prison and now he was in one. Everything changed so quickly.

"I got a call from Dylan Elementary."

"You did?"

"Yes, it was about a PSA job you applied for. Is that a para-professional position?"

She almost choked on the apple she had crammed in her mouth. "Yeah it is. They called you already?"

"Yeah, I have a friend from high school that works there, Kari. She works with behavioral kids. At least she did the last time I saw her but that was a couple of years ago."

"Behavioral kids? That seems like a rude way to describe them."

Gabby laughed. "No, no. That just means they have been diagnosed as having a behavioral diagnosis, like a disruptive behavior disorder. It doesn't describe the child, just the diagnosis. I worked with PCA's and aides at the shelter when I was there. Don't worry, you will catch on fast. You're so good with kids. They'll steal your heart. Who knows, you may end up adopting a couple, like me"

She laughed. "Gabby, you're a saint. I don't think I could have done what you did. Now you better not cancel on me, or I won't think you're a saint anymore."

. . .

AN HOUR LATER, she received a call and an interview was scheduled for the next day.

She walked into the office above the school garage and stepped into the office and only room on top. The grounds supervisor was in charge of the PSA's and their students but did not work in the schools at all. The burly man greeted her with a handshake.

"Mrs. Fredrickson, I'm Jim. I'm a huge supporter of your fundraiser. My wife and I have been going the past two years. Your speech sure inspired us and what your sister did…well, it's very rare. You must be so proud of her."

"My sister-in-law. She is pretty selfless, that's for sure." She was glad he was inspired by Gabby, but was this interview supposed to be about her?

"My daughter has both of the books she wrote." He shook is head. "I'm sorry, you must get sick of people always talking about it. Anyway, I would love for you to be a part of this great team here.You will be working at the Dylan Elementary. Go straight to the office Monday morning."

"I got the job?" He did not even ask her a question.

"Are you kidding me? You had the job the minute your showed up for the interview. You are just what we are looking for. I'm a good friend of Mr. Rivers and he said wonderful things about you. Congratulations." He stood up and walked back to his desk, dismissing her with his back turned.

She tried not to overthink the interview. Instead she focused on her future with the school. She was so excited to fill her life with helping children and making a difference. Gabby had changed so much when she cared for children at the shelter. She went on to become a mother and went to school to become a social worker. This was her calling, too. Gabby was just waiting until her kids got older to go back to work and Emily admired that. For Emily, this job meant more time with Irene because in a couple years she would be in Kindergarten at Dylan Elementary. Was this not every mother's dream job?

THE DRIVE from Side Lake to Hibbing for work only took twenty minutes. She needed to get used to the drive since there were no big stores in Side Lake, other than gas stations, a resort, and two restaurants. Everyone went to Hibbing or the city of Virginia for groceries and other shopping. Neither city was as big as Duluth where Gabby lived. It was a much bigger city with traffic and it was built on a hill next to Lake Superior. Northern Minnesota was not highly populated and consisted mainly of small towns, like Side Lake, with less than a thousand people, and lots of rural areas with lakes every few miles. The small cities were iron ore towns so the area was referred to as the Iron Range.

She walked in the front doors of the Dylan Elementary School and stopped. The school was long and narrow, and the ceilings were lower than she remembered in her elementary school. The walls, the ceiling, even the floors were white. Silver lines of big squares were drawn on the floor to help the children walk in a straight line.

A woman smiled at her. "Please go to the office."

The office secretary was away from her desk. One of the women standing in the hallway looked Emily up and down and turned in the opposite direction, a frown on her face like she was annoyed by her presence. Some welcome.

She looked down at her outfit. Was it all wrong? Had they heard about Matthew's problems already? Would they ever stop gossiping in Hibbing?

The other teacher in the hall was petite with a friendly smile. She approached her. "Excuse me, hi, my name is Emily

31

and I am a new PSA. I'm not sure where to go. I'm looking for Mrs. Eli. Do you know where her classroom is?"

"Straight to the lunchroom," the woman said as she watched the kids come in the door.

She did a double take. Was the teacher talking to her or the students?

The teacher turned back to Emily. "That was Liz Eli who just walked into the lunchroom, she has lunchroom duty this morning."

Oh great, the crabby lady was Mrs. Eli.

"The PSA's usually gather in Liz's room in the morning, and I'm sure they can help you. It's right down that long hallway there to the right. It's the first room on the left."

"Thank you so much, Mrs ... I'm sorry, I don't think I got your name."

"I'm Meghan. I'm a kindergarten teacher and my room is right here if you need anything. You should probably hurry before the bell rings. Great meeting you." She opened the door to help a small child struggling to get in.

"Thank you," Emily said.

There was only one adult woman in the room when she entered. The woman looked up with a smile. "You must be Emily, I'm Kari."

So this was the Kari Gabby told her about. "Hello Kari," she said. She shook Kari's hand.

Kari's red hair and blue eyes were a perfect combination. Her smile was warm and welcoming. This job might be the best decision she had made in a long time.

"I'm heading to the cafeteria where Liz is right now. If she gives you evil looks that's just the way she is, and it's not you, it's her. Honestly, I think that is the way her face looks, she can't help it. You'll be working with Anna, who is the sweetest little girl. She's on the spectrum and can become physical at times, but she's so cute. She struggles with cognitive skills and needs a lot of redirection. Where did you work before here?"

She did not want to say, but Kari seemed distracted as they headed down the hallway because she was busy saying hello to children and teachers passing them in the hallway. Kari said she was trying to keep an eye out for her student who sometimes liked to linger in the hallway instead of going right down to the cafeteria.

"When you say on the spectrum, what exactly does that mean?"

Kari laughed. "Oh, I'm sorry. It means she is autistic. Are you from the area?"

"No, but I've lived here for quite a while. Actually, I think you may know my sister-in-law, Gabriella Fredrickson?"

"Oh, Gabby. I haven't seen her in a couple of years. How is she? Where is she living now? I heard she got married."

"She's doing great, married with three kids. She lives in Duluth and is currently a stay-at-home mom."

"Wow, three kids, huh? That is unbelievable. How does she have three kids already? They all hers?"

Every seat in the lunchroom was packed with kids. Emily had to speak louder for Kari to hear her over their voices. "It's a long story."

"For next time. Hey look, there's Anna."

Kari pointed to a little girl wearing a pink snowsuit.

"You can introduce yourself and then walk her to her kindergarten class. They line up by grades so she will be first. I'm actually right down the hall in Meghan's room."

"Oh okay, I met her. She seems great." Was Mrs. Eli really not going to give her any training for the special need's child? She took two steps in the direction of Anna and then turned around. "So, what is the name of the teacher Anna has? And where exactly is the classroom?"

"Mr. K, just follow Anna, she knows where she's going.

Good luck!" she called out before quickly heading in the opposite direction toward her student.

She gulped then took a deep breath. Not one child looked up at her as she passed them and made her way to Anna. She kneeled down next to her. "You must be Anna. I'm ..." She wasn't sure if she should be Miss Emily or Mrs. Fredrickson or just Emily. "Emily."

A little boy interrupted her before Anna answered. "I'm Franklin, my mom named me after her favorite president of the United States, Franklin D. Roosevelt, and I had pizza for breakfast but I'm not supposed to tell anyone that."

Emily laughed. This definitely caught her off-guard. Here she was worried about what a bunch of young kids would think of her when really they just wanted her attention. Franklin reminded her of Gabby's daughter, Melanie. Although Melanie had cancer at a young age, she was always happy and rambling on about things. One time she even told Emily that her house smelled like pee, and Emily ended up buying a very expensive carpet cleaner because she could not get the smell out, according to Melanie. The smell made Melanie sick, and Emily did not want her to stop coming over. She treasured their time together and loved her random stories.

ANNA LOOKED at the wall instead of at her. "Are you my new teacher?"

"I sure am. I get to come to class with you."

"Yay!" Anna stood up and hugged her. "Why isn't Miss Patty here anymore?"

Oh crap. She should have tried the Miss before she gave Anna her name. Now how would she tell her to call her Miss Emily? She was not going to worry about it until she talked to Mrs. Eli. Was Mrs. Eli her boss or was Mr. K? Talk about being tossed into the ring. She should have asked more questions after they told her she was hired, but she was so excited and not thinking clearly. She would have to ask Kari more questions.

Anna walked in a single-file line with her class all the way down to her classroom. Emily reminded her to follow the silver line as she walked. She had to redirect her a couple of times for talking to Franklin, but it was only because she kept accidentally stepping on the back of his shoes, and he told her to stop. Anna seemed to have a hard time focusing on small tasks.

They entered the classroom where a rug with big square letters filled the floorspace.

The students turned a corner into the closet. The closet was huge and a wall separated the closet from the classroom. There were hooks on both sides and two doorways to get out, a doorway to the small bathroom, and a doorway that led to the outside with a big red exit sign above it.

Anna stood watching the other kids take off their winter clothes.

She dropped to her knees beside Anna and helped her take off her snowsuit. It took her much longer than the other kids to remove her winter clothes and only Franklin remained in the coat closet when she finally finished.

She took a peek inside Anna's backpack to make sure there was nothing she needed to take out. "Now hang up your backpack, Anna."

Anna complied.

Franklin sat down next to Anna in the closet. "Could you tie my shoe, please Miss Emily?"

Everyone was sitting around the carpet in a circle outside the closet, but the teacher had not come in yet. The kids were out of control, talking loudly, and one little boy was climbing under the table, doing what looked like the breast stroke on the floor. The loud voices made her impatient. Was this the way a kindergarten class was run? Were they this out of control or was it just the lack of supervision?

THE ROOM WENT quiet as a man's voice began reading names off. The students answered with hot or cold lunch and milk or no milk after their name was called.

Emily finished tying Franklin's shoe and followed Anna and Franklin out of the closet.

She looked up at the sound of the teacher's voice and choked back a gasp. Dawson was standing there where the teacher should be. He was staring at her. Her mouth dropped. Dawson Kersich was Mr. K? She never imagined Dawson capable of being a teacher, but even if she knew he was, what were the odds he was the teacher for the class she worked in? The only two people in this room and probably in this school who moved to Minnesota from Florida. He gave her a carpentry card with his name on it. Did he work both jobs? If he did, he sure had a lot of time on his hands. She shaded her eyes with her hand in the hopes he would not notice her, but she was pretty sure he already did when their eyes locked.

The talking stopped and Emily looked up as their eyes connected.

He grinned and stood up. "Boys and girls, we have a new friend with us today. Will you be helping Anna in my classroom now, Miss Emily?

She tried not stare directly into his eyes. "Yes."

"Okay, friends, let's all give Miss Emily a big Dylan Elementary welcome by saying welcome Emily as a class, okay? Here we go."

"Wel-come Em-il-ly," they all said in unison or tried and failed to say in unison.

She waved back. "Hello, class. I'm so excited to be here."

She never wanted to quit so badly on her first day at a new job as she did today. Would Dawson be her new boss? How could she face him and keep her secret? She had to focus on Anna, and not talk to him. He lives next to her and she has to work with him now? After all these years, this was too much all at once. Everywhere she went, he seemed to be. But it was February and they only had four months of school left. Then she would hopefully be out of his class forever and she could just hide in the cabin to avoid him.

His butt looked good in his brown slacks and half-zipped green sweater. She put her head down, not wanting him to catch her staring at his butt. She hated him for what he did, and she wasn't going to let it go that easily but he was so damn good looking.

As the day went on, she kept her back turned and looked away from him to avoid eye contact. Every now and then he would call her out in front of the class and ask, "Do you know what letter comes after j?" Or another time when he asked her if she knew any more words that rhymed with bat because the rest of the class could not think of anymore and she replied, "Fat."

Later on during story time, Anna let out a loud toot when the room was absolutely silent. Emily was surprised that no one even acknowledged it until Dawson mouthed, "excuse you," to her. She was sure all the kids would laugh but maybe they were too young to judge. She shook her head and laughed.

At lunch, Kari found her and stood next to her as she watched Anna eat.

"How's the day going so far?"

Dawson and the comments he spit at her flashed across her mind, but that was too personal to tell Kari the first day she met her. She did not want Kari to think she was a snob. "It's okay, I guess. Anna has been really good."

"It's called the honeymoon phase. Give it a week or two and she'll fall into her typical behavior patterns again. If she gets out of control and you need to leave the class, either have Mr. K call the office to get Liz to come help you, or walk Anna down to Liz's room. Don't be afraid to ask for help."

"Thank you. I still haven't met Liz ... Mrs. Eli?" She was not sure if she should call her by her first name right off the bat. Although everyone else seemed to call her Liz, she was not going to take the chance and piss her off. "Does she prefer to be called by her first name?"

"I call her Liz because I knew her before she was a teacher, even though I never really liked her. Some teachers I call by their professional name but I guess it depends. Do what you are comfortable with."

"It does seem weird to call them by their first names if I don't know them. When will I be seeing Mrs. Eli again?"

"She has lunch duty with us and should be coming in any minute. She will come and talk to you and let you know when it's your lunchtime. Oh and having a hot teacher like Mr. K helps to make the day go by fast, doesn't it?"

"Dawson? No, no I don't think he's hot," she said. Her voice was loud and defensive. "I mean, I just know Dawson from when we were kids, that's all. I don't think he's attractive."

Kari wrinkled up her eyebrows. "I thought he was from Georgia or something?"

Emily stuttered. "Actually it's Fa-- Fa-- Florida and ... um ...well we both grew up there and moved here. We ...had a mutual friend."

"Oh, what a small world," Kari said.

Kari glanced around the room and then moved closer to

whisper in Emily's ear. "I think Mrs. Eli has a crush on him so be careful not to be too friendly, if you know what I mean. She can be really evil if you get on her bad side."

Mrs. Eli came into the lunchroom and walked over to her with what looked like her resting bitch face. "I'm Mrs. Eli. I will be your supervisor. Do your job and there won't be any trouble, you understand? Any questions?'

Friendly as expected. "No questions. Nice to meet you."

"Your lunch is right after Anna's lunch. You bring her to my room and you'll have forty minutes. It's really not enough time to leave, but if you do, don't be late. Got it? Oh, and if you have any problems just come to my room, okay?"

She nodded and forced a smile. Mrs. Eli turned her back and made her way over to a table to yell at some kids for standing up. Her yell was a terrifying, deep voice, like the villain in a horror movie.

Emily leaned closer to Kari. "Quick question. Isn't Mrs. Eli married? I mean, with her being addressed as missus, it's weird she has a crush on Daw ... Mr. K."

"Newly divorced and keeping his last name. Rumor has it she has a cabin in Side Lake just a few doors down from Dawson. She got it in the divorce. Her first name is Liz. You can call her either."

"Oh great," she said under her breath. "Another unwanted neighbor." This relaxing move to the beach was becoming not so secluded and relaxing.

MARCH

CHAPTER 5

*D*ear Emily,
    I am so sorry for what I am, and what I've done to you and Irene. I never thought I would get back into drugs again. Although I love you so much, I know it's time to let you go. It's for the best. I need to focus on myself right now and my recovery. You and I both know this is what is best for Irene. She doesn't need a dad who is locked up in jail. Please don't visit me, and especially don't bring Irene to visit me because this is not a place for children and I will turn down the visit.

    You deserve better, and I love you and Irene, and I always will. Continue being the amazing mother you are. It is time for both of us to move on. Don't wait for me. I can't get better if we are still married. Please don't feel guilty. I love you with all of my heart, and I want you and Irene to be happy. Don't be stubborn, move on. You are better than this. This is what I need too.

    Love always,
    Matthew

. . .

LOVE ALWAYS, Matthew. What a joke. She tried calling him at the prison, but they said he could not receive phone calls because he was in segregation for fighting. Next came the knock at the door.

A sheriff stood there at Jillian's door. "Are you Emily Fredrickson?" he asked.

"Yes."

Was Matthew dead? But no, he handed her an envelope and said, "You have been served." Then she wished he was dead. The envelope contained divorce papers.

She burst into tears and sank to the floor. He did not love her anymore. He was divorcing her, whether she wanted a divorce or not. She meant nothing to him after all these years. He was too busy fighting in prison. Was he still doing drugs while he was in there? Could he get his hands-on drugs in a prison? Probably.

In a fit of anger, she slammed the kitchen cabinet.

Irene woke up crying from her nap. She had been sick, but her forehead was no longer hot, and her temperature read 98.9.

She held Irene against her shoulder and rocked her in the glider Matt's mom had given her right before Irene was born. It was an antique. Perhaps Destiny used to rock Matthew and Gabby in it when they were little. Matthew's dad had passed away while Destiny was pregnant with him. Was it hard for her to raise the kids without a father around? Jillian was around to help, but that was not the same Jillian said..

She held the papers out to Jillian.

"Is this what I think it is?"

Emily nodded.

"It's for the best, honey, you need to move on with your life."

"You knew about this?"

"I knew Gabby went to see him in prison, and I knew he wanted what was best for you and Irene."

"How could Gabby? She didn't even talk to me first."

Jillian touched her hand. "This is what's best for Matthew, too."

"Why does everyone think they know what is best for us? You guys aren't in our relationship. He needs help, he can't do it without me. I have to save him." He needed her, and Destiny would have wanted her to stand beside him through his recovery.

"It's what Matthew wants."

"But I know I can help him this time. I didn't pay enough attention to him. I can fix this, really, I can fix this." She put her head in her hands and cried.

"Sweet girl, this isn't your fault. What he did was his choice. He is an addict, and he can only move on and gain sobriety on his own. He needs this. You need this."

"But why didn't he call me and tell me what he was doing? He won't answer my calls, won't accept my letters, they were all returned. I just don't get it. He blames me, doesn't he?"

"No. No. And if he did, that wouldn't be your fault either."

"I expected this from Matthew but not Gabby. It feels like a stab in my back. Gabby should not have gotten involved."

"Please don't take this out on Gabby, she watched him fall and you crumble right with him. You would have done the same for her. See what happens and if it is right, you guys will end up together when he's better. It's for the best. Have we wronged you before?"

No, they had her best interests at heart, but she wanted to be a part of this decision. It was her life, after all. She was not a teenager, she was a grown adult.

"I need to talk to him face to face. For closure. Please let me do this."

Jillian nodded.

"What time are visiting hours?"

Jillian hesitated. "There aren't any today, but tomorrow you could make it after work. What about Gabby? She and the kids will be here, and I know she wanted to help you with the cabin."

"I'm still not happy with her, but I won't be too long. Will you watch Irene for me tomorrow?"

Jillian nodded. "We'll just stay at my house tomorrow then, okay?"

She agreed. She needed to see Matthew, needed to know if he was sure this was what he wanted.

"Em, what happens if he won't see you?"

"He will," she said. She would make sure of it.

SHE LEFT Irene with Jillian the next morning instead of taking her to daycare the day after a fever. Nor did she have any sick time since she had only been at her job for a few weeks.

Anna hugged her good morning. "Time for class, Anna."

She followed Anna into class, but her mind was on seeing Matthew at the prison. Anna was taking too long in the closet. She made her way into the closet, but stopped to help Franklin put his mittens and hat in his hood, and two others hang up their jackets. She even picked up a boot that was in the middle of the coat closet floor and set it to the side. She finally reached Anna, who was on the floor, sitting against the wall with all of her winter clothes on except one mitten that was thrown across the closet.

She squatted down to Anna's eye level. "Anna, what's going on, honey?"

Anna let out a grunt and crossed her arms tighter. She turned her head away.

"What's wrong? Would you like me to help you take your stuff off?"

"No!"

She turned her whole body away from Emily and faced the wall.

Was this what she had to look forward to when Irene got older? Damn Matthew for forcing her to do this on her own. She did not need a man in her life, but a father would be helpful. Would he continue on this road of using after he got out? Was he ever going to be sober again? He would if she had anything to do with it. If he would let her.

The day was not looking good, and it had hardly begun. She silently prayed for a miracle to help get Anna up. Her thick Hibbing sweatshirt and long-sleeved shirt were choking her. Sweat beads collected on her forehead and she felt like passing out. She took a drink from her water bottle and sat crisscross applesauce as kindergarten called it, on the floor in front of Anna.

"We can spend the whole day in the closet, but we're going to miss out on lunch call, and the morning dance time, and learning the alphabet and—"

Anna's bottom lip puffed out. "I no like school."

Those big brown eyes made her want to pick Anna up and hug her, but she could not enable this kind of behavior.

"I don't know why you don't like coming to school, sweetheart. You have so many friends, and you get to do so many fun things, and you get to see me," she said in a high voice but quietly so the whole classroom could not hear her.

Anna sprawled on the closet floor like she was getting ready to make snow angels. "I miss my mommy.

Dawson peeked around the corner. "Anna, Emily, is everything okay back here?"

"It's fine, Anna is just having a hard time. She misses her mom."

Dawson brought his six foot-two stature down to a two-foot squatting position on the floor next to her. She could not place his scent, but he smelled so good he put her in a trance-like state. She hated how she leaned closer and involuntarily took in deep breaths just to get more of it. She pulled back.

Dawson looked down at Anna. "The floor is really dirty, buddy. Why don't you take your stuff off so you don't get hot, and come and sit in a circle with us. The whole class misses you, and I miss you."

The one-on-one attention did it. Anna sat up, smitten with her teacher. "But I want my mom."

"I'll tell you what, why don't we sing our morning songs, do the pledge of allegiance, and then if you still really miss your mom, we can talk about that then, okay? How does that sound?"

She stood up and rubbed away the tears in her eyes. "Okay."

Emily helped Anna take off her jacket and snow pants, and tucked her hat and mittens into the hood. Anna was wearing a Minnie Mouse sweatshirt, red leggings with white polka-dots, and black Mary Jane shoes with white socks.

She would have to ask Anna's mom where she bought the cute clothes. Maybe they had the same outfit in Irene's size.

When she was little, her mother bought her polka-dot bibs with a silver-glittered shirt and ballet slippers for her birthday. She wore the outfit three days in a row before her mom caught on and told her she was going to be called a ragamuffin at school if she wore it again. When she came home from school the next day, her mother had given the outfit away to the poor. "You're not responsible enough to have it," she had said. Her mom cared too much about what others thought. Her life and her family's lives revolved around what others might think. What about what Emily wanted?

Anna made her way to the carpet for the morning songs, pledge of allegiance, and then to their table spots before she had another meltdown. She wanted to color while Dawson was talking, and Emily had to take her crayons away from her, which led to her throwing a pencil at sweet little Franklin. He started crying and then Anna got down on the floor and began screaming and yelling, "I want my mom. You promised! Liar!"

Emily did everything she could to calm Anna. She told her big girls don't cry and that if she had a really good day she would push Anna on the swing at lunchtime. Swinging was Anna's favorite thing to do at recess. But nothing worked. The crying got worse and she ran out of ideas.

Dawson came over. "Is there something I can do to help?"

She glared at him. "I have it handled."

"I'm sure you do," he said. He went over to the intercom and pushed the white button on the wall.

A voice came over the intercom. "Yes, Mr. Kersich?"

"Hi, Amy, can you send Mrs. Eli to my room please? Anna is having a hard time and may need some assistance."

"Right away."

She scowled at Dawson. How dare he call down the mean supervisor when she just needed more time to help Anna calm down? "Come on, Anna, let's go for a walk, okay? That will make you feel better. Will you come for a walk with me?" She did not move.

The door open and in walked Mrs. Eli. She smiled sweetly at Dawson. "Hello, class, is your teacher behaving?"

She swung her hips and stared into Dawson's eyes, practically drooling over him while Anna screamed and cried and kicked the table.

Mrs. Eli gave Emily a devil glare and shook her head at her. "Excuse me, Miss Emily. Please go stand by the door."

Emily did as she was told. Maybe Mrs. Eli would have a hard time getting Anna out of the room, too. This was an impossible job. Who did she think she was?

Mrs. Eli whispered something to Anna and continued to whisper for a minute or two, and then helped Anna up as if she had just fallen on the ground and needed help to get to her feet. Mrs. Eli followed Anna out of the room. Anna stopped and reached for Mrs. Eli's hand. Unbelievable.

"Have a great day, everyone," Mrs. Eli said to the class. "Make sure you listen to Mr. K, he's really smart and knows what he's talking about."

She waved to the class. "Anna, you wave, too."

Anna did so with a smile, no sign of the tantrum that distracted the whole class.

Emily followed them in absolute disbelief as Anna and Mrs. Eli talked about Easter and what the Easter bunny was going to bring Anna. Mrs. Eli talked about her own kids and what they both asked for. They laughed and Mrs. Eli even had to shush Anna when she laughed too loudly in the hallway while students were trying to work in the classrooms.

Emily passed the door that led outside. A part of her wanted to walk out the door and never come back, but the adult side of her told her to swallow her pride and learn from this.

In the classroom, Mrs. Eli had Anna working on writing the letter A. Emily was not sure what to do so she sat next to Anna. An hour went by and Mrs. Eli was still working with Anna and she had not done anything but watch them. Mrs. Eli did not address or acknowledge she was sitting right there until lunchtime. "Get Anna's lunch from the lunchroom and bring it back to her. She will not be eating in the cafeteria today."

On her lunch break, Emily went into the teacher's lounge and ate her peanut butter and jelly sandwich on white, a bag of Cheetos, and a strawberry Bubbly. She had the same lunchtime as the second-grade teachers. She quickly learned the second-grade teachers were cliquey and good friends with Mrs. Eli. They reminded her of high schoolers.

Miss Johnson, first name Jan, was blonde and wore too much makeup, false eyelashes, and tight shirts to show off her rather large breasts. She was single with no kids, but had a long-time boyfriend. He proposed to her twice, but she said she was too afraid he would want kids if she married him. She was rude and judgmental and always had to be right.

"She's bitter and leader of the pack," Kari whispered, following her gaze.

"Why's she bitter?"

Kari shrugged. "For some reason she thinks she has to be perfect, and it makes her blunt and rude. No one stands up to her because they're worried she'll treat them even worse."

Emily laughed. "Like a queen bee.

Addie, Mrs. Edward, was another second-grade teacher. She was married and did not talk about herself, but for some reason she was best friends with Jan. Addie was always telling jokes and had everyone laughing at lunchtime. When she talked, she would look at everyone in the room equally, including Emily and Kari, unlike Jan who would talk as if her three friends were the only ones in the room. Whenever Emily spoke up, Jan would talk louder and cut her off. Ellen, Mrs. Zell, teacher number three always agreed with everyone else. She was superficial, like Jan, but not pretty like Jan. She liked to talk about how great she was with makeup.

"Never mind her," Kari said. "Her husband sells drugs and she ignores it as long as he buys her designer clothes with the money. Her husband mows lawns in the summer and shovels snow in the winter."

"That's his real job?"

Kari nodded. "She's been trying to have kids for like five years but can't get pregnant, which is actually sad."

"Maybe if she had kids, she would be kinder," Emily said.

Then there was Mrs. Eli. She would come in about halfway through their lunch to chat on her way to the bathroom. She was at least ten years older than the other teachers in her little clique. She never said much, but she always sat as far away from Emily as she could.

All the other teachers she met were so kind, but and real, a variety of ages. The other teachers were more like teachers and less like teenage girls who thought popularity in their late twenties was a thing.

She began dreading lunchtime. On days when it was not too cold she went for a walk with Kari around the block just to avoid them, but that was not often since it was always cold this time of year.

EMILY WALKED in the lunchroom and heard Jan telling the other women about Matthew. Jan must have thought she was outside walking since she and Kari were both late. Although Jan was evil, she would never say such things to her face or she would have by now.

She walked into the gym and cried and cried, not her proudest moment. When her lunchtime was up, embarrassed and hungry, she went back to Mrs. Eli's room and acted like everything was fine. Jan and the other women were not worth another tear. She had to be strong for Irene and strong around family. Vulnerability was a sure way to show bullies they were getting to her. She learned that back in high school.

The rest of the day, Emily spent watching Mrs. Eli work with Anna. Other kids came into the room to work with Mrs. Eli. "Would you please move, Miss Emily, so one of the children can sit next to Anna at the table?"

Emily could feel her face growing hot and the breath being forced out of her lungs.

Mrs. Eli acted as if she was not in the room, and if she tried to interact with Anna, Mrs. Eli would stand directly in front of Emily or send her to get something from the office or another classroom. Why was she even there if she was not needed? If she would not teach her the skills to do this on her own or at least let her work with Anna a little bit, there was no reason for her to even be there.

Emily watched the clock until the bell finally rang at 2:15. She walked straight to the exit. She met Kari in the hallway and stopped to talk with her, but she just wanted to run away.

Kari opened the outside door and they stepped into the cold. "How you doing? Is everything okay? I saw you were in Mrs. Eli's room most of the day, that is never good.

The cold and heavy air seeped down Emily's spine, leaving her with chills. March was supposed to be warmer, but the cold would not let up. The parking lot was full of cars from teachers and parents who came early to pick up their kids. She wiggled her numb toes and hopped up and down to keep warm. Kari was becoming a good friend. She had to tell Kari what happened, even if she froze while doing it.

"Yeah, Anna had a behavior and of course Mr. K called Mrs. Eli to save the day. I don't know how she did it, but she got Anna to settle down. With just a few whispers in her ear, Anna was jumping and skipping out the door." Replaying it made her angry all over again.

She shoved her hands in the pockets of her wool coat and scrunched up her shoulders.

"Yeah, she does that, and don't get me wrong she is good at helping kids when they have meltdowns, but there is always a motive. She likes to swoop in and save the day and be the best without teaching us how to handle it." Kari sighed. "We don't get along and haven't in years. I'm blunt with her, and I don't take her crap, nor should you."

"Yeah, she didn't even acknowledge me in her room. I felt useless and dumb. I walked into the break room today, and those teachers were all talking crap about me." She did not want to talk about Matthew right now. She did not want to explain to Kari what he had done in case Kari had not heard yet.

Kari put her hand on Emily's shoulder. "Don't let her or the rest of the clique make you feel that way. It's all part of their plan to beat you down to make them feel better. Liz wants to look better by making you feel like you can't handle your job and that you need her. You're prettier than she is, and she's probably jealous you're in Mr. K's class. Just watch your back with her. She has an in with the principal, and if she doesn't like you, they'll get you moved to another school or write you up. I'm not kidding. One PSA had an anxiety attack during our summer training when she found out she was going to have Liz as her supervisor, and she ended up quitting. Don't let her get to you."

"Does Mr. K see right through her?"

Kari laughed as she unlocked her car door. "No, she has most of the teachers fooled except the older teachers who have been around for a while. Meghan, too, doesn't feed into it. Meghan is so great. She isn't afraid to stand up to her and put her in her place. Everyone will eventually find out she's fake. I just go to work, do my job, and go home. This job is hard when you have to deal with people like her, but I've stayed at Dylan Elementary because of the kids. I love the kids I work with, and the teachers are mainly great, too, except that group. They aren't so bad when you are alone with them. Just give it a chance and remember, she's nasty because her home life sucks. No one acts that way unless they have a reason. See you tomorrow and keep your head up."

CHAPTER 6

"

Matthew

*M*atthew was lifting weights when the guard popped his head into the weight room.

"What's up?" Matthew said.

The small white room was so quiet. No music, only grunts from the other men working out, and the wonderful smell of body odor that never went away.

"You have a visitor."

Matthew sat up. Was Gabby here to see him? He sent the divorce papers to Emily. Maybe she was here to see him. His palms began to sweat. "Is it my wife?"

"They didn't say. You will have to come and find out, I guess."

Matt looked down at his stretched-out tank top and black sweat pants. "Like this?"

He lifted his arm and sniffed his right armpit. Not too

bad. If his visitor was Gabby, it was no big deal. She'd give him crap, but it didn't really matter. But if it was Emily ...

"Yeah, man. If it's her, hear her out. You still haven't talked to her, have you?"

Matthew talked to the guard, John, a lot about his situation with Emily, and he gave him great advice. His heart was torn. He toweled off his wet hair and shook his head. If Emily saw his beat-up face she would be angry and think he had not changed at all. But it was far from his fault. He was jumped in the hallway and did not want to fight back in fear of getting a longer sentence.

The guard patted him down. He led Matthew to the wall where he had him turn around to pat down his backside. He gave him the nod, and Matthew took a deep breath and held it. He saw the back of her head as he rounded the doorway.

She turned in his direction, and their eyes locked. He lost his breath for a second. Just breathe. Her hair looked blonder than her normal strawberry blonde. No, stop it. Gabriella was right, he needed to let her go. He hesitated and almost walked right back out. Then he remembered what John said. He could not let her go if he kept avoiding her.

"Matthew?"

She mouthed his name. Chills ran through every nerve in his body. His legs went limp, and he put his hand on the back of the chair to support his weight. He waited until the nausea passed, then walked over and sat down next to her. He ran his fingers through his hair and tried not to get lost in her eyes. His heartbeat was all over the place, and he gave up trying to control it.

"Your ... face ... what happened?" She reached out to touch his face but stopped short. "Who did this to you?"

He moved his hand to block her view of his bruises. She was always treating him like a child. He could handle himself. Why did she always have to act like his mother? "It was just a misunderstanding. Everything is fine now. Promise."

She shook her head as if she was shaking him from her mind. "I'm sorry, but you look terrible. I worry so much about you, and I had no idea what it was like here. They're supposed to keep you safe."

She had tears in her eyes. Was he that repulsive to look at? He picked at his nails under the table. "I can take care of myself. It really isn't that bad." He sounded like a jerk so he added, "How's Irene?"

"Irene's good, she misses you."

Her eyes lingered a little too long on his arms and chest. A blush heat crawled up his neck. "And you?"

She looked down at the table. The divorce paperwork was in front of her.

"Well, I was fired from my job. No one wants to work with me because of what you did, and I thought it was the end of the world. Then I got hired as a PSA in Dylan Elementary School, and I was moving forward until I received this paperwork from you without even a heads up. You owe me an explanation. I came all the way here to get closure."

He chewed on his lip. "I'm sorry."

"I really don't understand you. I know you're afraid to talk to me about getting divorced. I came here today to sign this paperwork in front of you just like you want me to. And ..."

"And?" Matthew said.

He tried to read her expression, but he no longer knew her. She wanted this, she did not come to fight for him. She came to discuss the divorce, not to yell at him out of passion and anger. Everything had changed so fast.

"I'm going for full custody of Irene."

His hands opened up in front of him, revealing his battered face. "You can't, please don't."

"It's what's best for her, I'm sorry. I'm not trying to take her away from you, and I never will, this is just until you get your life straightened out."

"But, Em, I've been going to therapy, I want help. I love Irene, don't do this. Please don't do this."

She signed the paperwork in front of him and shoved it back into the manila envelope. "You can have her when Jillian or Gabby are with you. You did this. It's going to take some time for you to get the help you need, and I'm not going to let you fool me again or worse, hurt her."

"Damn it, Emily, I love you."

And just like that he could not take it back. It was a Freudian slip, diarrhea of the mouth. There was no covering up his emotions.

She stared at him with tears in her eyes, then stood up and walked away. "Goodbye, Matthew."

He watched as a guard stopped her before she exited. "Are you okay? I overheard the swearing and wanted to make sure everything is okay here."

"It's fine, sir, just fine. It's over so you have absolutely nothing to worry about. Excuse me," she said, without even a glance back in his direction.

CHAPTER 7

Emily

*E*mily slammed the door on her car. Luckily the damage was minimal when she was hit on the highway so she had no problem driving it. How dare he tell her he loved her after sending her divorce papers? Was this just a joke to him? She threw the divorce papers in the back seat even though a part of her wanted to rip them up, but what good would that do? Someone beat the crap out of him. His face was all stitched up and black and blue, his eye swollen, and his lip puffy. He looked horrible and he gave her a minimal explanation. And how did he find the time to get so ripped while in prison? Did he lift weights all day? With her luck he would get out of jail, get sober, look better than he ever had, and be healthier and find a woman immediately. Was she doing the right thing?

She leaned her head against the headrest. Yes, she was

doing the right thing. She needed to do this for her and for her daughter.

SHE REACHED Jillian's house after the long drive home.

"Mommy!"

She hugged Irene and helped her with her struggle into her too-tight jacket. Irene was growing so fast. She would have to get her another one before winter was over. She zipped up the snowsuit and grabbed her pink boots.

Irene's lip puckered. "I want daddy."

"I know, sweetheart. He'll be back before we know it. Let's get your boots on now because Melanie is waiting for you at the rec center and so is Ben and Auntie."

"I want daddy!"

This time she screamed it in Emily's face.

"Don't cry. Daddy loves you. How about I see if daddy can call you next weekend? How does that sound?"

She nodded her head. "Yeah!"

"Okay, let's go sledding."

That was easy. She was so used to Anna, where nothing seemed to work, although Anna was listening to her more and more as the days went on. It was almost April now and Anna seemed more comfortable with her, but she would probably forget everything during the summer break.

The sledding hill at the Side Lake Recreation Center was packed with people. The weather had turned a bit warmer. Kids without hats were building jumps to go down on their sleds.

Gabby, in her red hat and jacket, was racing Melanie and Ben up the hill but failing miserably.

Gabby was taking a leave of absence at work to raise her kids and that meant she could come up north to visit often.

Emily gave her a wave and they waved back. Ben yelled

something out as he came up the hill. They finally reached the top.

Melanie gave Irene a big hug. "Hi Irene." She turned to Emily. "Auntie Emily, can I go down the hill with Irene? I promise I'll be really careful with her."

"Are you sure?" Gabby said.

"Yeah, that's fine," she said. "Just don't go too fast, okay. Keep your boots out of the sled to drag them so you can control the speed."

Ben took a running head start and jumped on the orange saucer. He landed on his belly and flew headfirst down the hill.

"Be careful, Ben!" Gabriella said. "Boys, I swear he's going to give me a heart attack."

"Are you ready?" Emily said to the girls.

They nodded. She gave them a gentle push. They laughed all the way down the hill.

"How are you holding up?" Gabby said once the kids were far enough down the hill not to hear them.

"I'm honestly a little angry that you got involved with Matthew and me. Why did you go all the way to the prison to push him to divorce me?"

"I know I should've asked you first, but I knew you'd say no. This is best for everyone involved, and I knew the two of you would never do it without a push. You need a fresh start."

Emily placed her gloved hands on her hips. "That really wasn't your place, Gabby, and you know it."

"I'm sorry I upset you. Next time I'll ask, I promise," she said, drawing a Catholic cross over her heart with her finger.

"My gosh, Gabby, there isn't going to be a next time." Was she saying she thought Emily was going to get divorced again or get back with Matthew? She could not be sure.

"You know what I mean. I promise I did it with a pure heart."

Gabby gave her a pouty lip and they both started laughing. It was hard to stay mad at Gabby.

"Well, I signed the divorce papers in front of him at the prison today. He looks terrible by the way."

"I know and I'm proud of you. I'm sure it wasn't easy," she said. "He's my brother and I love him, but he needs to grow up. I'm sick and tired of watching him string you along for the ride. I had to do something."

"I know, you and Jillian always have our best interests at heart, even if you did act like a real jerk doing what you did."

"A huge jerk. So how are things? How are you really doing? You enjoying the cabin?"

Gabby glanced at the kids to make sure they were still doing okay and Emily's eyes followed. The kids left their sleds at the bottom of the hill and trudged through the snow until they reached the playground. Irene was way behind, but Melanie went back to help her.

"I'm not really sure what I think about cabin life yet, but I'm glad I have somewhere to go other than the house we shared together."

"You like your new job with the hot ex?"

"Gabby, I'm still married, you know. I literally just signed the paperwork, it's not like it could even be official yet. Plus Dawson is kind of annoying and full of himself anyway. He drives me absolutely insane, and I can't seem to get away from him."

Gabby grinned. "I hope I get to meet him. You know I need a face to go with the name."

"Be serious, Gabby. It's too soon for you to meet him. We aren't even a thing. I do hate that I have to see him every day at work, but I'm grateful to have a job."

"I know you are trying to change the subject, but how are you doing with money?"

"I'm not going to lie, I worry about money and how I'm going to pay the bills. Not that the money is bad at my job, but I don't get a paycheck all summer. It's going to take some getting used to."

"You'll get through this, and if you need any help you know I'm here for you."

"I can't take money from my friends, you know that. I had a really good job with great pay and then Hibbing happened. Irene and I are stuck paying for the mistakes Matthew made."

Gabby shook her head. "What they did to you isn't cool, but people are just ignorant in small towns. I know you think the people around here are mean to anyone who didn't grow up in Hibbing but they do warm up. They protect their own and they get scared when they hear about drugs. I think Side Lake is really going to help you see how awesome northern Minnesota really is. Just promise you'll keep an open mind."

"Easy for you to say, you grew up here."

"Well you may work in Hibbing and shop in Hibbing, but you are a Sidelaker now, living on Greenrock Road and on one long chain of beautiful lakes."

"It is really nice, even if I do have a neighbor who drives me crazy."

Gabby squinted down the hill. "A hot neighbor," she said under hear breath.

Emily hit her shoulder and Gabby laughed.

"It doesn't look like the kids are coming back so maybe we should go to them."

A car door shut behind them. She turned around. Mrs. Eli and her children were coming toward the hill.

"Hi," she said.

Mrs. Eli looked away and guided her daughter and son away from Emily. Franklin's arms were wrapped around

63

Mrs. Eli's waist. Franklin Eli, he was her son and she just now put it together. Ellen and Jan followed close behind. Mrs. Eli whispered something to Ellen and she looked at Emily and started laughing. She bent over and whispered something to Jan. Jan did not laugh. Instead, she glared in Emily's direction. If Jan were to smile or laugh she would probably have a heart attack.

"Do you know them?" Gabby whispered.

"That's my supervisor and her teacher friends. They think they are the coolest kids in school."

"What does that mean? Don't they realize high school is over?"

"They aren't even worth the thought. They're truly the mean girls, and Mrs. Eli is head over heels for Dawson," Emily said.

"I really need to meet this Dawson."

Emily picked up some snow, rolled it up, and smiled as she held it behind her head.

Gabby scrambled to get out of reach but the snow was too deep. "Don't you dare!"

Emily threw it and hit her on top of the head. The snowball broke and fell apart on Gabby's face and hair.

Gabby wiped her face and packed a snowball. She threw it at Emily, but missed. She bent down to pick up another one. "This means war!"

They ran around throwing snowballs at each other, Ben joined in right away and Melanie was right behind him. Irene picked up some snow and threw it but her snowball did not make it more than a foot before it fell apart. Emily hurried over to teach her to roll the snowballs.

They played until Jillian came to pick up the kids for their slumber party.

"Remember, you can't have a snowball fight like this in Florida. Minnesota is so much better," Gabby said.

Emilyloved growing up in Florida and Gabby was probably sick of hearing it. The sunshine, the beaches, summer all year long.

"Nah, in Florida you can throw sand," Emily said.

"That sounds like a terrible idea."

"At least it isn't frozen water."

"Touche."

THEY PULLED into the driveway as Dawson finished shoveling her sidewalks.

"Is that him?" Gabby said pointing. "Did he just shovel your sidewalks?"

Emily sighed. "Yes. He was probably just bored. I suppose you're going to meet him now, aren't you?"

"Oh you know it, girl."

Gabby was racing across the driveway. Emily followed, not even trying to stop her because she knew nothing could hold her back when she was determined. She debated sneaking in the back door, but that would probably lead to Gabby telling him to come in. She was on a mission for Emily to forget about Matthew, no matter how uncomfortable for Emily.

"You must be Dawson, I'm Gabby, Emily's friend. Emily was just telling me she was going to invite you in for a drink.

She glared at Gabby but put on a fake smile for Dawson. "Sure I did."

He glanced at her, a question in his eyes. "That's okay, I don't want to intrude. I think Emily gets enough of me at school, and I'm her neighbor now. I don't want to be a bother."

"Are you kidding me? You just shoveled her sidewalks and plowed her driveway," Gabby said. "We aren't taking no for an answer. Are we Emily?"

JULY 2008

* * *

CHAPTER 8

Emily

The day she and Jordan arrived in Duluth over a decade ago, the air was hot and humid, but not as hot and humid as Florida. Within a week, Emily found a job bagging groceries at SuperOne on the West side of Duluth. They no longer had to sleep in their car. They found an apartment above a company called Electric Systems that was within walking distance to her job.

Jordan was hired at the gas station and worked midnights, which was hard for her at first but she quickly grew to love the city and all it had to offer. Some days when Jordan was sleeping, she would go to Canal Park, sit in the sand, and watch the waves beat against the lake walk. It reminded her of home. She would buy ice cream down the street at Cold Stone Creamery and people watch.

Her thoughts always turned to her dad and sister because they were the only two left in Florida. How were they doing after losing her mother? She texted her sister, Jamie, all the time because Jamie understood what it was like to be far from home now that she was living in San Francisco, but she never talked to her sister, Lindsay. They were just too different.

She made a few friends at work, but Jordan insisted she did not have time for friends and that people from Minnesota were not good people. She did not understand why he felt that way, but to avoid fighting she never told him when she went for coffee with Victoria or to Barnes and Noble with Kate. Books filled her heart with joy and she could escape on an adventure with each read.

One day she and Jordan went fishing on the shore of Lake Superior. She tried jumping in, but the water was freezing cold even in August.

"You're a wimp. Quit being a baby," Jordan said.

She scrambled across the slippery rocks to get in the water, but slipped and banged her knee. "Ow!"

Jordan laughed. "Quit overreacting." He dove under a wave.

She limped her way out of the water and sat in the sand to take a closer look at her injured knee. A black-and-blue bruise was puffing up. She pushed at her knee cap, and it slipped out of her grasp. She bit her lip to keep from screaming.

"Jordan, I need to go to the emergency room."

"Calm down, Em. Suck it up, you're fine."

She tried to get up and fell back to the ground. Her arm hit against her chest. Odd, her breasts were a lot more tender than they had ever been. The pain in her knee receded in her mind as she thought back to the last time she had her period. A month, maybe two, before she left Florida. She was probably pregnant. The withdraw method was not fail-proof, but Jordan refused to use condoms. He said it cut off the circulation so why even have sex if they had to put a full rain suit on it? She could not afford birth control pills, and the diaphragm never seemed to be in the right place.

Would Jordan be upset? Did they have enough money to take care of a child? They were struggling to survive as it was, and Jordan spent all their extra money on fishing and camping gear.

"Jordan, I'm going to the doctor to get my knee checked."

He dove under water and did not hear her. He came up and shook water off his hair. "Wow, this is refreshing." He ran up the shore, and over the huge rocks as if they were on fire. He almost lost his balance on the last rock. He jumped onto the sand and did a summersault.

She tried to stand, but failed. "Are you okay?"

"Yes, I don't sit and complain over a little injury like you. Are you ready to come swimming, or are you just going to sit there and complain the rest of the day?"

"My knee, it—"

He stood and waved his arms. "Over here, guys! I didn't think you guys were going to show."

He grabbed a towel to wipe off his chest and strode over to a group of people. The overpowering smell of a skunk filled her nostrils and forced her to put all her weight on the other leg and stand up. She turned around to see Jordan with a pipe in his mouth and a guy holding the lighter in place for him. A beautiful blonde woman with scraggly hair and little makeup stood close to Jordan. She reminded Emily of a California surfer girl. The woman squeezed Jordan's lack of muscles and leaned her head against him intimately.

Emily ignored the pain as she focused on walking toward them. "Hello, I'm Emily," she said. Her eyes challenged the blonde.

"Emily, these are the guys, John, Joe, Landon, and Marley," Jordan said.

As he said Marley, he winked at the blonde, and her eyes were locked with his.

He referred to them as the guys, but Marley was definitely not a guy with her bright yellow low-cut bikini and neon green cover up. Her bright pink lipstick and wind-blown hair made her instantly insecure.

She stared at Jordan, trying to read his expression. Was he into this girl? Was he no longer into her? Was she not pretty enough for him? Skinny enough?

"We've heard so much about you," Marley said with a big smile. Jordan stared at Marley as if Emily was not there.

"That's funny, I've heard absolutely nothing about you," she said.

This was enough to snap Jordan out of his trance. "Sure I've mentioned Marley, she's just one of the guys."

Marley looked upset and uncomfortable. She twirled her hair around her perfectly manicured finger and snapped her gum.

"Excuse me, but Jordan would you mind driving me to the clinic? I seem to have sprained my knee."

Jordan let out a deep groan. "But babe, the guys just got here."

"Jordan, I can't walk, this cannot wait."

He rolled his eyes and turned his body toward the guys. "I'm sorry, I'll be right back. The water is perfect and enough to wake you right up. Don't leave without me."

Emily limped behind him. Jordan didn't seem to care. He was steps ahead of her and stomping his feet. "Hey Jordan, could you help me?"

He threw up his hands and let out a loud groan. He glanced back at her and shook his head. "You're really a pain in the butt, you know that? You just wanted to take me away from my friends. You're fine."

He yanked on her arm as he threw it over his shoulder.

He was thin and not very strong, which threw his balance off. "You really need to lose some weight, you feel quite ... thick."

She gasped and looked down at her stomach. She had struggled to put on her jean shorts this week. "Jordan, I think I'm pregnant."

He stood up taller and dropped her arm.

She fell to the ground.

He stared down at her and ignored her cry of pain. "What did you just say?"

He kicked her in the knee and sent a strong jolt of pain into her bad knee. The pain became excruciating.

"What did you just say to me?"

"You heard me."

"You dumb blonde, you did this on purpose, didn't you?"

"No, Jordan, no. You think I wanted to get pregnant? How can we raise a baby? We can't afford a baby."

She tried to stand up again. He followed behind her as she limped her way to the car.

"You're getting an abortion."

She gasped. How could he be so cruel? "I'm not getting an abortion. This is our baby, Jordan."

She tucked her head into the car and lifted her bad leg with her arm.

He did not say a word for the rest of the drive. When they pulled up in front of the clinic, she glanced at him. "You don't want to come in with me, do you?"

He laughed under his breath. It was a snarky laugh, full of anger and blame. "Go. Go to the doctor. I'm going back to see the guys. Obviously my opinion doesn't matter to you anyway."

She had seen him mean before, but even this was unexpected. She slammed the door and made her way into the clinic. He sped off, his wheels screeching as he drove away. She stared at the car until she could no longer see it.

She was scared when she told the doctor she might be pregnant. The test came back negative, she had put on weight and there was no reason why. "Are you under a lot of stress?" the doctor asked her. The answer was yes. Jordan would be so relieved to find out she was not pregnant.

CHAPTER 9

Emily

*A*lthough she loved her job, Emily had a hard time getting to work the next morning. She did not want to continually be reminded of her past every time she saw Dawson. Dawson's big smile and positive attitude annoyed her because she really wanted to hate him. It was just easier that way. Anna was in a mood, and she had to redirect her too many times to take her winter clothes off. She had a meltdown because she wanted to keep her boots on. When Anna threw her boot at Franklin, Emily lost all her patience.

"We don't throw things at other people, Anna. You could have hurt Franklin. Say you're sorry."

Anna looked down at the ground, hands at her sides, not making any eye contact. "No."

"Anna, when we do something wrong we apologize. How would you feel if Franklin threw a shoe at you?"

Anna moved so her back was to Emily.

"I'm going to sit with friends while we take the morning attendance and then dance. When you're ready to apologize to Franklin, you can come out and join us."

Now that she knew Franklin was Mrs. Eli's son, she was more worried about Anna's actions toward him. She did not want Mrs. Eli to think she was letting Anna pick on him. It would give her another reason to yell at her for not doing her job.

She made her way to the chair behind Anna's spot on the floor.

Anna peeked out from the closet.

Dawson whispered in Emily's ear. "Are you trying to see if she will come out on her own?"

"Yes. I'm ignoring her in the hope that she will change her attitude."

"Good luck. Let me know if there is anything I can do to help," he said and walked away.

When it was time for the class to move to their tables, Anna still had not come out of the closet. She did not want to involve Mrs. Eli and risk spending the whole day in her room watching her bond with Anna when she was the one trying to build that connection with her. Mrs. Eli would swoop in and take over again. She prayed Dawson would not interfere and call Mrs. Eli. How was he so blind?

Dawson showed the students how to write the letter E. "Okay, let's all practice the letter E now,

He walked over to her. "Is there something I can do to help? Should I call Mrs. Eli?"

Well, at least he finally asked. But she was unsure of what to do. Tears welled in her eyes. "I don't know."

"Hey, it's okay. We don't have to call her. I know she can be a bit much. We'll figure it out together, okay?"

Dawson's dark curly hair hung down his face and landed on his eyebrow above his left eye. The curl was almost long enough to cover his beautiful eyes. She smiled at him through her tears.

"Why don't you run to the bathroom, okay?"

She nodded and made her way down the hall. Why did she cry here of all places? Her pale skin tended to become blotchy red when she cried. She needed to get it together.

On her way back to the classroom, she saw Jan. Jan smirked at her and kept walking, Emily looked down. She brushed it off and tried not to think about it. When she entered the classroom, Anna was sitting in her seat. She waved to Emily

She gave Dawson a questioning look. He shrugged his shoulders and continued talking about words that started with the letter E.

Anna continued to struggle throughout the day, but she was able to handle all the little problems. Anna refused to put on her shoes after playing outside at recess. She pulled on Lillian's hair during story time, and she cried when Emily would not let her sit on her lap in the library.

Emily pushed past it because Anna's behaviors were not as bad as in the morning. Dawson was there to help, which gave her the confidence to handle Anna on her own.

At the end of the day, Mrs. Eli came in to talk to Dawson. She flipped her hair behind her shoulder and put her hand on her hip as she laughed like a hyena.

Emily hid her smirk.

Dawson did not seem irritated by the conversation, and he nodded his head a lot. He did not turn around, as if he had forgotten he had a full class of five-year-old kids relying on him. Mrs. Eli talked to him for about five minutes. The kids decided they could talk too, and the noise level rose.

She had to try something to settle the class. "Hands on your head.

The room went silent, and they followed her lead.

"Hands on your shoulders. Now hands on your toes."

They continued to follow her lead. She led them all to the front of the room and settled them in a circle. "Let's read a story, shall we?"

The kids quieted and all eyes were on her.

Dawson looked her way, and Mrs. Eli's gazed in her direction, too.

Her face heated up. "And the porcupine got his quills back," she said and closed the book.

Franklin's hand shot up in the air. "Why did the porcupine lose his quills anyway?"

She opened her mouth to answer him, but Anna got up and ran as fast as she could for the door.

She chased after Anna and stepped in front to cut her off. As lightly as she could, she grabbed Anna's shoulders. "Where do you think you're going, little lady?" she said with a smile.

"I wanna go home."

"Me too, but we have to wait for Mr. K to tell us to get our snow pants on because it's really cold outside, and we don't want to freeze, do we?"

Anna looked as if she was really thinking about that. She frowned. "No."

She let Emily lead her back to the class.

"Okay, everyone, it's time to get ready to go home. Take your work out of your cubbies and put it in your backpacks," Dawson said.

A sense of relief washed over her. The day was almost done.

"Line up in your rows."

He waved to her when he called Anna's row. "Miss Emily, can I speak to you for a minute?"

"What's going on?"

"What you did today to keep the kids occupied, I really appreciate it. You're really good with kids, you know that?"

"Thanks," she said.

"What is your plan after school?"

She laughed. "I may have to take up smoking or drinking, I think."

He laughed. "Yeah, it was a rough day. I hope you don't think I'm crossing the line here, but I'd like to invite you to my house for coffee after school and apologize for crashing your day with your friend Gabby."

She side-eyed him, unsure of how to reply to his invitation.

"I don't bite," he whispered. He called the next row to get ready.

"As long as you know we're just co-workers getting together to chat. We need to get along if we're going to continue working together."

"Come on, we used to be best friends and you're married, right? Emily, I'm the same guy as the friend you grew up with. I really haven't changed that much. But I need you to let me explain what happened that day. I hurt you, I see that now. Let me explain. Please."

"I'll think about it."

"That's all I'm asking."

The way he said it was so cocky. He knew she would listen, and he knew what he did wrong. He was not that guy she grew up with. She did not know him at all anymore. Her best friend changed when he started falling for every girl within a five-foot radius of him.

CHAPTER 10

orking with five-year-olds all day was physically and mentally exhausting, but having Emily with him was the highlight of his days. She was so good with the kids and so smart. The way she took over the classroom while he talked to Liz about Franklin's social issues was mind blowing. He felt terrible when she almost broke down in class and he had to send her to the bathroom. It took him a lot of self-control not to put his arms around her and tell her everything was going to be okay, like the old days. He needed to make it right with her. He hoped she was serious about his coffee invitation and would show up so he could show her he was the same guy she grew up with. Her best friend. She could only turn down his invitation so many times before his ego was ruined.

She was married and he respected that. Sure he was still in love with her after all of these years, but he would rather be her friend than nothing at all. Just having her back in his life was life changing for him. He had been through so much in the last few years. He had lost a part of himself as his world fell apart. He needed to share his feelings with her, she had always been his person.

As Dawson drove out to the lake after school, he thought back thirteen years ago when he moved to Minnesota to live with his cousin, Jordan, and Emily. Not a good move. He still wanted Emily. He drank almost every night to keep from thinking about her, but nothing worked. Emily had put on a little weight and looked so good. She seemed less confident though, which broke his heart. She needed to be with someone who cared for her, loved her, and treated her the way she should be treated, like a lady. She was going downhill with Jordan by her side.

He got lost in her eyes and had to turn away when he was around her. He never should have moved to Duluth, but at the time he just wanted to be near her. He sat on his hands when he was around her to keep from reaching out and touching her. He longed for the kiss they shared back in Florida after her mother died. Her lips had been so soft and luscious. He could no longer deny his love for her, and he felt terrible about it. He should have fought for her when he had the chance. Jordan was not good enough for her. He was always ditching her to hang out with his friends.

One night Jordan tried to convince him to come out with them.

"I'm up for a night out. Is Emily coming, too?"

"It's just the guys, man. No girlfriends allowed," Jordan said.

Dawson went inside to change. Emily was in the living room knitting.

"Aw, you're making me a sweater so I can enjoy my first winter in the tundra?"

Emily laughed. "No. I'm making myself a scarf. It may be

summer but winter comes so fast, just wait and see. What are you guys up to?"

Of course Jordan neglected to tell her they were going out. He did not seem to care about Emily, but it was none of his business.

"Um, going out for a couple beers with the guys, I guess. What are you up to tonight?"

"This is it. I'll probably watch some chick flicks and finish knitting my scarf."

He wanted to stay with her, take her out rock climbing in Canal Park or down to the Harbor to watch the boats come in, but she was not his girl. Not anymore. How could he come in and swoop up his cousin's girlfriend? Jordan had graciously invited him to stay with them for a couple of months until he moved into the dorms on campus, and that was not the best way to repay him.

"I--"

"It's fine, go out and have fun with the guys. I probably won't wait up."

He was pretty sure he heard hostility in her voice. He wished more than anything he could just stay home, but he did not trust himself alone with her. "I'll see you tomorrow, then."

They ended up at some college party that was on the East side of the city. Jordan introduced him to *The Guys* who happened to be three guys and a girl who smoked a whole lot of weed. After a few drinks, he loosened up and enjoyed himself. Lincoln Park was blaring and they were jumping around like animals and taking keg shots upside down. Jordan was the star of the party. Women were hanging all over him, but he had his eyes on only one, Marley. Just as he suspected, Jordan was having sex with Marley. It was so obvious.

Jordan ripped open Marley's shirt in front of the crowd,

exposing her bright pink bra and cleavage. He grabbed the bottle of vodka and turned it upside down, soaking her, and then he tossed the bottle. It crashed into the counter behind him and broke into a hundred pieces. The crowd cheered. The guy who was renting the house yelled out, "I got it," and held a broom above his head. The crowd erupted in loud cheers once again. They chanted Jordan's name as he began motor boating Marley.

Dawson was disgusted and he had seen enough. How dare Jordan do that to Emily? He snuck out of the party and called a cab.

The light was still on in the living room when he reached the apartment. His buzz gave him some liquid courage. Emily needed to know what was going on.

He struggled with his key in the lock. He was about to give up and knock when Emily opened the door.

She laughed. "What the hell, Dawson? Put the key in and turn, it's not that hard."

"Oh you little--" He chased her around the apartment and finally cornered her by the couch.

She pretend-scowled and shook her finger. "You know I don't like to be tickled, you know I don't. Don't you dare."

He laughed louder and tackled her on the couch. She laughed so hard. He could not remember the last time he heard her unique giggle. It made him smile and dig his fingers in deeper.

"Seriously, Dawson! I'm going to pee my pants!"

"I'm sorry, I didn't mean to--"

She jumped on top of him, and held his hands behind his back then poked him in the chest and stomach with her pointer finger. He could have gotten away without a prob-lem, but where was the fun in that? He laughed and wiggled because it tickled but also hurt as she poked him, but so what? He wanted this moment to last forever. She stopped and her face was just inches from his. He wanted to lift his head and grab those lips he'd dreamed about for so long.

She tucked a dangling strand of hair behind her ear, but didn't try to move away from him. "That will teach you not to mess with me. Do you give up?"

He nodded and they both got up and sat down next to each other on the couch, both out of breath. He came home early because he wanted to be honest with her. He knew it was going to hurt her, but he would rather live on the streets then let Jordan treat her this way. "Emily, there's something I need to tell you."

She stopped watching television and turned to him. "Is everything okay? If it was about the couch, I'm sorry. I didn't mean for to go that far. You're Jordan's best friend."

He grabbed her hand to stop her. "No, no. That was fine. Better than fine. I just have to tell you something, and you're probably going to be upset."

She rolled her eyes. "Is this about the guys?"

"Kind of."

"Um, let me guess it's about Jordan and Marley?"

She knew? What could he say? Why didn't she do anything about it? "Yeah, I left the party because they were um ... well I guess out of respect for you."

She moved closer and held onto his arm with both of her hands. "You have always been so real, you know that. Honest and kind. The truth is Jordan does not think I know about Marley, but I do. The late nights and the smell of Peach from Bath and Body Works on him every night when he gets home. The late phone calls when he sneaks into the living room to talk to her. He obsesses about the guys and to tell you the truth, I don't care. I have nowhere to go right now so please, Dawson, please don't judge me."

He rested his forehead against hers, and they sat there for quite a while, tears streaming down her face. She pulled away and went into the kitchen and fetched a bottle of Jordan's whisky. They took turns chugging it, and they laughed and laughed.

She took a swig of the bottle, held it in her mouth, and then she kissed him, transferring the whisky into his mouth with her tongue. Although her lips were firmly pressed against his, it went spraying all over both of them and up his nose, which made them laugh even harder. Once the burning in his nose subsided, he used his sleeve to wipe up the whisky on her face. Their eyes met, and they began tearing their clothes off and throwing them across the room.

He could see two of her. He blinked his eyes, but he was more drunk than he thought. He had waited his whole life for this moment, and he was so dizzy he could not focus on her. He wanted to wait until he was sober enough to remember every detail, but he might miss his chance. He kissed her gently and made his way down her naked body until she stopped him.

"Dawson Kersich, take me now or never," she said.

So he did. That was a night he would never forget. Her body was smooth and soft. She was everything he dreamed she would be, and he wanted the moment to last forever. They took it slow and as they both finished together, he lay down next to her. Reality struck his fuzzy brain. This relationship could not continue unless she left Jordan, and he would have to keep his distance until then.

HE PUSHED the old memories down and pulled his car into his driveway. She walked up the stairs to his front door a couple minutes later. She actually came this time. Would she want flavored cream in her coffee? His wife always liked hers with French vanilla creamer, but all he had now was skim milk.

"You really live here all by yourself?" she said when he opened the door.

"Sure do. Why don't you have a seat? I'm just brewing up fresh coffee. Do you like medium roast?"

She nodded. "What made you decide to buy such a gigantic house just for you?"

"It wasn't just me when we bought it."

Emily raised an eyebrow. "Oh really, was there a missus? Did you two break up or is she hiding out somewhere? You didn't cheat on her did you?"

Dawson grinned. "None of the above. Cream?"

She shook her head. "That makes no sense, which is it?"

"Let's not talk about her right now, okay?"

She looked confused, waiting for an explanation he was not ready to give. He did not want to chase her off the first second he had her alone in his house. She was still beautiful and perfect in every way. And he still wanted her. She never knew he had cut her off because he loved her.

"Sounds like someone is a little bitter. I like this girl already."

"Let's talk about Gabby. How do the two of you know each other?"

"She's my sister-in-law. My husband's sister." Emily took a sip of the hot coffee and winced.

"Careful, it's hot. She's your sister-in-law?"

Her sister-in-law was trying to set them up, but that made no sense because Emily was married to her brother. He had to be getting something wrong and he needed to figure it out. But first, he wanted Emily to stop hating him.

"Yes ... well kind of."

"What does kind of mean?"

Her eyes turned distant, lost in thought. "I just signed our divorce papers."

He remained silent. Pressing her for details was not a good idea, but she would tell him when she was ready.

She brought her coffee cup to her mouth and took a sip. "He did some things that weren't very good."

"Don't we all?"

She took another drink of coffee and looked into his eyes. "He's in prison."

"That's not what I was expecting. He didn't kill anyone, did he?"

He meant for this to be a joke but once he said it he wanted to bite his tongue.

"No, he didn't kill anyone. He's an addict and he thought it would be okay to be all cracked out at our daughter's birthday party. It was hell."

She was sharing her personal life with him. Was she finally starting to trust him? "Wow, I don't even know what to say. And after all what you went through with your mom."

"I still love him, Dawson. He was the one who wanted the divorce. I know I can help him, I just wish he would give me the chance but he won't talk to me. I went to see him at the prison yesterday, and I signed the papers he had filed. As I was leaving do you know what he said to me?"

Dawson waited for her to continue and shook his head.

"He said he loved me. It is crazy coming from a guy who had just sent me divorce papers. Gabby and his aunt both wanted me to divorce him. They pretty much talked him into it, which makes my blood boil but I know they mean well. His aunt is even letting me stay here rent-free until I get on my feet, but I know it's just because she wants me to leave Matthew. Weird, right?"

"They sound like some great people," he said. "Looking out for you."

She took a deep breath and shook her head. "Enough

about me. Tell me about you. Where in the hell did you get this amazing home? I can't imagine how much it cost."

"My wife came from a lot of money, and she was a pharmacist."

He shuddered. His memories still hurt too much. He blinked away the tears.

"What happened if you don't mind me asking?"

He got up and grabbed her coffee cup. "More?"

"Yes, please," she said. "If you don't want to talk about it, you don't have to. I don't mean to pry."

"It's not that, I don't really talk about it. It still hurts too much."

She raised an eyebrow. "Another time?"

He wanted to tell her, wanted her to know there were no more secrets.

"My wife's name was Bobby. She was an amazing woman and a pharmacist, like I said, in Duluth. We were married at the Gray Salon Ballroom, which is probably the most beautiful place I have ever seen. She was kind and beautiful." No he could not do it. Best to change the subject. "I went through some hard times after you left and after what I did to you. Jordan never found out we slept together, and I talked him out of trying to find you. I convinced him you went back to Florida and he believed me. He moved back to Florida with Marley and they got married, had kids. He's different now, he's grown up."

She touched his arm. "Tell me more about your wife, please."

He took a deep breath and willed his heart to slow down. "I was finally happy. Bobby and I got pregnant and during her maternity leave we decided to buy this cabin and spend our summer and fall out here. Her parents bought it for us as a wedding present actually. She was almost nine months pregnant when we moved in, due any moment. A few days later she had some uncomfortable gas, but we had no idea she was in labor. By the time we got to the hospital, the baby didn't have a heartbeat. Bobby went in for emergency surgery, but she was in shock. She didn't make it. They both didn't make it. "

He put his head in his hands and walked to the window to stare out at the lake.

"Oh wow, I had no idea. I'm so sorry. They both ..."

He nodded. "We worked so hard to get the nursery done before the baby's arrival. We were going to name him Tyler after my dad." He turned around to read her reaction. Finally talking about it felt good. His family and friends knew not to bring it up. He never allowed it."I sold the pharmacy and moved into this place and started applying for teaching jobs."

"How long ago?" she said.

"It'll be five years now on July thirtieth."

She joined him at the window. He felt the warmth of her body with each stroke of her hand on his back.

"I wish I could have been here for you. I'm so sorry. When I found my mother that day I thought there could never be anything close to as bad but ..."

He turned around and grabbed her arms. "Don't you dare think this is worse than what you went through. That was horrible when you found her. I felt so useless when I couldn't take away your pain. The day she died and I held you all night, do you know what I was thinking?" He shouldn't be so forward with her when they finally started talking again but he needed to say it.

"What?"

"I was wishing I could hold you in my arms forever. You were my best friend and I felt horrible Jordan wasn't there but I was so glad I was. If that isn't selfish, I don't know what is."

"I know, because I felt the same way."

He needed to ask her now, or he might never again get the opportunity. "I've been wondering about something since I was a teenager, and I really need to know the answer."

"Okay."

"Why did you leave me for Jordan? What did he have that I didn't?"

Not a question she probably wanted to answer, but one thing he learned from losing his wife was that life was too short for regrets about what he should have said.

"Remember that day on Ft Myers beach with your family? My mom made me take my sister Lindsey with me. Remember how I had to stay under that stupid umbrella due to the third degree burns and blisters on my shoulders?"

"Yeah, I remember. That was the day you left with Jordan."

He would never forget that day. He had punched a brick wall and broke his hand when she left with Jordan. He was so angry. He had racked his brain for years as to why she did not want him and what went wrong.

"Well, you were flirting with Lindsey because she beat you in that stupid castle-building contest, remember?"

How could she think he was flirting with her sister? "I wasn't flirting with her. She was your sister, and I only had eyes for you, whether you knew that or not."

Lindsey's bathing suit was skimpy and he may have been wondering if he was going to get a glimpse at her nipple considering he was young and curious. But he never had a crush on Lindsey.

"Trust me, you were flirting. Jordan sat down next to me and I was pissed at you. You were splashing Lindsey and I was so mad. I left with him to get back at you, but then I fell for him. I thought you were dating Lindsey, I just thought the two of you were hiding it. I was jealous and I wanted to punish you."

"I may have been a hormonal teenaged boy but Lindsey

wasn't exactly the dating type. Sorry to say that. I'm sure she's grown up and much different now, but back then she developed fast and she was kind of known as easy."

"Oh I know, I remember all too well. I'm pretty sure she hasn't changed much."

He gazed at her. Emily's face was clear and even without any makeup. She was the most beautiful woman he had ever seen in a different way than his wife. Bobby was more of a woman who wore makeup and had to be perfect at all times. He loved her that way. She had perfect posture, and she was the smartest person he knew. She was his best friend, and he loved her so much. But Emily was the girl next door. Humble and beautiful and sweet.

She cared more about helping the world than she did her makeup and nails. She cared about the planet and children who were in the foster care system. She took a stand against what was wrong in the world. Her biggest problem was the battle within herself and the fact that she could not save her mom and now her ex-husband. He knew what he had to do. He had to fight for her or risk losing her again forever.

APRIL

CHAPTER 11

Emily

Something changed after their coffee date. She felt a sense of sadness for Dawson's pain. Maybe he was not so terrible. He had been through a lot and losing his wife and child seemed to really change him. Maybe they could be friends again.

She went home about seven to meet Jillian and Irene. Irene talked to her dad, but a three-year-old talking on the phone was not ideal for anyone involved. She said hi and kept running away from the phone. Emily had to chase her around with the cell phone and make her talk.

Jillian laughed. " Matthew is pretty good about it, but his feelings are likely a bit hurt."

Irene needed to see her dad. "Do you think I should take her to see Matthew at prison even though he said not to?"

"No, not at all. Besides, he gets out in May. She'll be okay. I mean she probably won't even remember him being gone."

She squinted at Emily. "You aren't thinking about getting back with him are you?"

She closed her eyes. Why did everyone tell her what to do? "He's my husband, Jillian. You, being his aunt, should understand better than anyone."

"I'm sorry, sweetheart. I really should keep my opinions to myself, I just don't want to see you get hurt again."

THE SNOW WAS FINALLY MELTING and the playground at the school was a swamp, but the trail leading inside the school from the park was solid ice from the daily foot traffic. Anna came to school that morning without boots on, which meant she was not allowed to play outside. To children this was the end of the world. When everyone else was getting dressed to play outside, Emily had to take Anna aside and explain why she could not go outside. Anna kicked and screamed and had the biggest meltdown Emily had ever witnessed.

"Hey kids, let's put our clothes on out here," Dawson said.

Dawson led the kids into the hallway earlier than usual to get away from Anna's screaming fit. Emily was covering her ears, unsure of how to handle the situation.

A voice called out to her. "Miss Emily, where are you?"

Was Mrs. Eli coming in to save the day? "In the closet."

"I talked to Mr. K in the hall, He said all this screaming is because you think Anna can't go outside without boots."

"I'm just enforcing the school policy."

It was not Mrs. Eli, it was Jan who came in with a pair of pink boots. "You should have asked about spare boots. This is torturing the poor girl. You really need to get better at your job."

She stepped in front of Emily, which threw her off balance since she was squatting in front of Anna.

"Don't cry, it's okay sweet girl. There's no reason for you to stay inside. Mrs. Johnson is here to save the day!" Jan said.

She pressed her lips together to keep from laughing.

Anna wiped her tears and laughed, her eyes filled with happiness.

"Now go play outside," Jan said.

Emily ignored Jan. She was not even worth the battle. Jan was a teacher and she was just a PSA. Starting problems would not get her anywhere. She walked around Jan to stop Anna from running down the hallway.

Jan stood up and held onto her sleeve.

"I have to go, I have to be with Anna."

"I don't know who you think you are, but stay away from Dawson. If not, I will have you fired. You have no idea who you are messing with here. He belongs to Liz."

"Are you threatening me?"

She had no time to wait for an answer as Anna bolted out of the room. She chased after her, but she was nowhere in sight. She picked up her pace and sprinted down the hall.

"Slow down, Mrs. Fredrickson," the principal said.

No one called her Mrs. Fredrickson here. This meant only one thing. Someone told the principal about Matthew and she wanted Emily to know she knew.

She took her lunch to the gym and ate by herself. Why did she have to sleep with Dawson all those years ago? It had complicated everything.

She thought back to the day after she slept with Dawson a little over twelve years ago, she had felt sick to her stomach. She wanted to remember why they ended up the way they did. Yes, she had a crush on him and he was not just some guy, he was her childhood best friend. He was the man she thought she was going to marry someday. But he was her boyfriend's cousin, and she slept with him in the bed she shared with her boyfriend that night. She did not love Jordan anymore, and she had been trying to find a way out, but sleeping with Dawson was not the answer. Jordan never hit her again, but maybe that was because even the passion between them was gone. Jordan's infidelity with Marley hurt at first but it was easier for her to get away if he had someone else. He would likely just let her go.

She thought all day about what to do. She needed a plan. Nor would she sleep with Dawson again until they moved out. She would talk to him that night when they were alone and let him know she wanted to be with him. She was sure he felt the same way. No one knew Dawson like she did, or so she thought.

That night every lane at the bowling alley was packed. She called Jordan. "Hey, the alley is packed. We should try the one by the mall."

"I'll meet you there."

As she pulled in she spotted a blonde with heavy eyeliner and a killer body in tight pants and a tight shirt. She was talking to Jordan and Dawson through the passenger window.

Emily parked her car and walked over to their car.

"Thanks, guys!" the woman said and blew a kiss at them. "Call me sometime, handsome," she said to Dawson. "Even better, call me tonight because I'm having an after bar at my house."

The woman turned to her. "Hello." She skipped her way to her navy-blue Oldsmobile..

She watched the woman pull away just to make sure she was really gone.

Dawson opened his car door.

"What was that all about?" she said.

"The girl's car died so we jumped it for her like good people," he said.

"Except she wanted Dawson's dick," Jordan said. He mimicked the woman. "Hey Dawson, call me, let's party."

Her stomach twisted and she bent over and puked right there in the parking lot.

"Gross, what the hell, Emily," Jordan said.

His disgusted look did not hurt her at all. He was literally making her ill. She needed to get him alone because the long-awaited conversation was killing her. It was so over.

She felt much better and they bowled three games, but she could not stand being around Jordan any longer. He was rude and made sexist comments and crude remarks at woman he thought unattractive. He was drinking heavily, and tripping and dropping the ball. She was sure they were going to get kicked out of the place.

Jordan went to the bathroom, and when he came back Emily and Dawson had turned in their bowling shoes and put all eight of the bowling balls away. Jordan had six because he kept blaming the bad bowling balls on why he had so many gutter balls.

Jordan came running up from behind Dawson, pulled his head back, and put him in the headlock. Dawson was much stronger so he pulled Jordan off of him.

Dawson growled. "What the hell, man.

He held up a familiar blue card. "I'm sorry, I'm just excited. Guess who I just called?"

"You didn't." Dawson grabbed the card from his hand. "How the hell did you get this anyway?"

"I saw you throw it in the trash, and I decided it was time for you to get laid so I called her. I got her address. We're going to her party. She said there are already people there so let's go."

She stood there, obviously forgotten. Dawson never gave

her the side eye or anything. Maybe he regretted what happened between them. He was pretty drunk. Was she so stupid to think he really had feelings for her after all this time?

"Alright, but I'm driving," Dawson said.

When they got to the party, she actually had a good time. A country band was playing and the slutty woman's house was huge. They played quarters and she dominated, hardly even having to take a drink. Jordan was getting wasted so she tried to find Dawson. He had gone to get them beers, but he had been gone a long time.

Marley showed up and found Jordan right away. Emily snuck away and searched the house for Dawson. She walked past the woman who invited them. "I love your party and the band is pretty cool."

The woman nodded.

She needed to pee before she talked to Dawson. "Where's the bathroom?"

"Just down the hall, you can't miss it."

She opened doors in the hallway since the women never told her which one was the bathroom. She opened the last door in the hallway. Had the woman sent her in the wrong direction on purpose? She turned on the light and that is when she saw the beautiful blonde on her knees, peeking around Dawson.

Dawson glanced back and saw her. His face paled. "Em, sorry."

That's all he could say? Sorry? She closed the door. He was just like the rest of the men she knew. She was another chick to him. She would not be talking to him anytime soon. She was a fool for believing he was different.

Over the next couple of weeks, Dawson tried talking to her, but she just walked away and ignored him. Six weeks later she finally broke up with Jordan. He laughed in her face and said, "It's about time you got out so Marley can move in."

His nastiness should have hurt her but it didn't. Leaving without saying goodbye to Dawson was not that hard because she was still disgusted with him. Hopefully it would hurt him as much as he hurt her, but she was highly doubtful.

THAT WAS the last time she saw him until he saved her life on the side of the road.

EASTER BREAK

* * *

CHAPTER 12

Emily

*E*aster was just around the corner and Emily was looking forward to a long weekend away from work. She loved Anna, but she needed to relax and enjoy some time with her family. Holidays were special because they were all about family and celebration, taking time to be with those she loved. She could not imagine what it was like for Dawson around the holidays without his wife and child. Did he do anything for Easter? His parents were so far away. Did he dread the holidays? Was he going to be alone? How weird that she was more concerned about Dawson than Matthew, who was spending his Easter in prison.

Anna sat well through most of the day in class, although she was still interrupting quite a bit during story time. Dawson was so patient with her when she interrupted him. He involved her more and made her feel special, yet he was firm when he needed to be.

During free-time, Anna was on the floor doing a puzzle

with Franklin. Emily sat at the small table and colored. Dawson pulled up a chair and sat next to her.

"What you doing?"

She stared at his perfect dimpled chin and strong jawline. "Just coloring."

"I haven't colored in ages. Anna sure looks happy, huh?"

Anna was now dancing around the room with a bright pink boa around her neck and twirling it in the air.

"I don't really understand why we make kids sit and be quiet. It is like society puts this unrealistic expectations on these young kids, but yet people with outspoken voices stand out and are said to have big personalities. In my opinion some kids just can't. Look at how happy she is," Emily said, nodding in Anna's direction.

Dawson's eyes followed her glance. "I never thought about it that way, but it is true. It kind of seems like a way to make the teachers happy more than really teach the children, doesn't it?"

"Can you imagine letting them run wild?" She laughed at the thought.

"This place would be a disaster," he agreed.

He put his hand on hers and squeezed it before getting up to tell the class to clean up. He turned on the cleanup song and left her longing for another touch.

SHE WALKED Anna to the bus and gave her a hug goodbye at the end of the day. Did Anna have a good home life? Her clothes were always clean, her Friday folder always came back on Monday morning, and Anna's mother or father always answered the notes she sent home with Anna. A lot of kids in the class did not have that. Maybe their parents worked and were too busy, or maybe they had family issues that made small tasks difficult. She just wished life could be easier for Anna. She was eccentric and did not blend in with the others due to obstacles from her special needs. To Emily, she was unique and when happy she had a contagious smile.

When Emily went inside to grab her purse, Dawson was standing by the door looking at the television and waiting for buses to be called. All the kids were quiet as they watched *Wild Kratts*.

"Hey you, any plans for Easter break?" Dawson said, like he read her mind.

"Going to Duluth to hang out with Gabby and their family. How about you?"

She would feel obligated to invite him along if he did not have plans. Although he was a friend, that would be weird. It was her husband's family after all. But how awful to sit in that huge house all by himself thinking about how the Easter Bunny would never bring his child candy.

"My mom and dad are coming up from Florida for the weekend. Just for two days. They worry about me being all alone but I really don't mind it. I usually curl up with a good book or binge Netflix."

She laughed. "For some reason, I can't imagine you sitting down and watching television all day. You were always the active type."

Back in high school, Dawson was out of touch with television. The only time he sat down to watch anything was when he watched the news for a half hour or *Ghost* with Emily. He was always busy with sports or homework, but most of the time he lived at the beach and would usually drag her along with him.

She jumped when her phone buzzed. She pulled it out, and startled she dropped it. Dawson picked it up and handed it to her. She grabbed it in one fast motion. Lindsey showed up on the screen. She silenced it and put it in her pocket.

He raised an eyebrow. "Was that your sister, Lindsey?"

"Yeah. I gotta go, have a good weekend."

She was not ready to tell him she'd been avoiding her sister and most of her family for years. It hurt too much to think about staying in contact with them after losing her mother, and now it had been so long she would not know what to say. She had not been to Florida since before Irene was born, and she had no plans to go back again anytime soon. She did send pictures of her family to her dad each Christmas, but with no return address. She was so close to Jamie, but after everything that happened between them in San Francisco, she could not bear to talk to her again. It brought back too much pain. But her sisters and dad never gave up. They still called around the holidays. She always planned on calling them back, but she never worked up the courage to dial their numbers or pick up their calls. Her family made her remember her past mistakes, and she was trying so hard to forget them.

THE SNOW WAS FINALLY MELTING, though the trees were bare, and the grass was brown and dead. The streets were even brown from the salt spread by the salt trucks to de-ice the streets. Usually a street sweeper came by in May or June and swept the ugliness from the streets. Spring was muddy and ugly, yet everyone waited anxiously for the cold to go away. By Easter they all wore pastel colors and even white.

On Saturday she and Irene met Gabby and her family at the Miller Hill Mall in Duluth to get pictures taken with the Easter Bunny. But Irene cried big tears when she saw the bunny. Nor would she let Melanie hold her. Emily ended up in the picture of the Easter bunny holding a crying Irene. The pictures were printed right away, and she laughed because Irene was staring at the bunny and her lip was quivering. Her big tears and blotchy face made for a good story in the years to come.

"Let me see that photo again. It's the funniest thing ever," Melanie said.

Ben and Melanie were so well behaved. They were always helping Gabby take care of their little sister, Tia, who was a year old now.

Melanie was so excited to see Emily and Irene, she could not stop talking.

"AUNTIE EMILY, my scans came back clear again, the cancer hasn't come back," Melanie said.

She hugged the little girl. "I knew they would."

She picked up Irene. "And my mom and I are writing another book."

"That is really great. I can't wait to read it," Emily said.

Melanie beamed.

Emily smiled. This Melanie was so different from the lifeless little girl in the hospital just two years ago. At one point, she did not think Melanie was going to make it. Melanie was only five years old at the time. Her brother, Ben, had been so angry with the world back then. They now had the love and stability they never had before.

"I want a video game!" Ben said.

Gabby kneeled down in front of him. "Now Ben, is it Christmas? Your birthday? Do you have a job we don't know about?"

Ben shook his head, his lip stuck out in an impressive pout.

"When it's your birthday or you have a job, let me know and we will talk about it, okay."

Ben calmed right down. Gabby handled his tantrum so well. She needed to take notes.

Travis looked at a pouty Ben and said, "How about a piggy back ride to the car instead?"

Ben's face lit up. "Yeah!"

Melanie looked up at Gabby. "Mommy, what about me? Will you give me one, too?"

"I'm sorry, but I have your little sister in my arms right now."

"I can set Irene down and carry her. Irene can hold my hand and walk, can't you honey?" Emily said.

Irene nodded.

"Hop like a bunny!" Melanie demanded as she jumped on her mom's back.

TRAVIS TOOK Melanie and Ben four-wheeling while Gabby and Emily spent half of Saturday prepping for Easter dinner. They drank Merlot and danced around the kitchen while the little ones napped.

She loved Gabby's home and called it a mansion. She remembered the first time Gabby stayed with Travis when this was just his house. The size of his house and all his money made her back off. Emily loved that about Gabby. She was not a money chaser. She was humble and everything she had, she truly appreciated.

"Lindsey called me today," Emily said. She needed to talk about it. It was Easter and her family was always on her mind.

Gabby gave her a side eye. "Did you answer?"

"No, but in my defense, I was talking to Dawson, and I was still in school."

"What is the story with that guy, anyway?"

"We're just friends."

. . .

GABBY FROWNED. "Oh, Em. I know you don't want me to get involved, but I think you two are each other's drugs. You keep getting back together, but it just makes everything worse."

Why did it always come back to this? She needed to change the subject. "Just drop it, okay? I feel like we keep going in circles and I don't want to fight about it anymore."

Gabby nudged her. "You know I'm on your side, but I do have a difficult time keeping my mouth shut. You'd be the same."

"Emily!"

"Did you hear that? It sounded like someone just said my name."

They turned around to find Jillian in the kitchen with her arms open. "Now who wants an apple pie, and where are my grandchildren?"

Jillian's daughter had gotten into trouble when she was a teenager. It broke Jillian's heart. When her daughter met a good man and they moved to Europe, Jillian let her go. She had bonded with Emily over missing their family.

Jillian kissed the top of her head. "How are you doing, girl?"

As if on cue, her phone rang. Jamie showed on the screen.

"Well, are you going to answer it?"

She switched it to silent and grabbed a seltzer water out of the fridge. "I'll call her back later."

Gabby shook her head. "Sure you will."

EASTER MORNING WAS MAGICAL. THE KIDS' baskets held a bit of candy, a stuffed animal, a DVD, and small toys and a kite. Olivia, Travis's mom, came over around eight in the morning to help cook Easter dinner. Jillian and Olivia did not always seem to see eye-to-eye, but Gabby was very good at calming them down or diverting the conversation to the children. Olivia liked to talk about Olivia and Olivia alone. She meant well, but was very opinionated.

Travis's dad, Casey, showed up at noon, the time dinner was scheduled. He was tall, dark, and handsome, like an older version of Travis. He was a lawyer and looked like one. He talked so sophisticated and even showed up in a suit and tie. Gabby wasn't kidding when she said he was a lady's man. That smile was a killer.

Jillian's husband arrived shortly after dinner started. He was a traveling salesman for a medical equipment company, so he was gone most of the time but that seemed to work out for him and Jillian. They liked their space, and Jillian loved her grandma time.

They sat around the table with the food in the center. Emily found herself missing her sisters and her father.

"We need to bless our food," Olivia said. "But I'm not the one to do it." That was just like Olivia to demand something but expect someone else to do it.

"I'll say grace," Jillian said. "Dear Heavenly Father, thank you so much for bringing all of us together here on this beautiful Easter day to celebrate our family and our religious beliefs. Please help Matthew as he continues to recover. Also, I pray for my dear sister and brother-in-law who are truly missed here at this table today. We know they are in good hands with you, Amen."

"THAT WAS BEAUTIFUL," Olivia said. She reached her hand over and placed it on top of Jillian's on the table. "Simple but beautiful. Dez and Bryan will forever live on in our hearts."

Everyone agreed. For their first Easter without Matthew,

it was probably one of the best holidays she could remember. Irene did not even seem to notice her father's absence. Maybe she was starting to get used to it.

MAY

CHAPTER 13

Dawson

*H*e went to school at six in the morning to prepare his lessons for the day but no matter how hard he tried, he could not focus. He kept thinking about Emily. He loved spending every day at school with her. She was so beautiful and smart and so great with the kids, especially Anna. It was May and soon her ex-husband would be released from prison. She said she wanted to make things work with him and Matthew was the father of her daughter. He dreamed about what it would be like to be with Emily. His timing was always terrible.

He never stopped loving Emily or thinking about her through the years. He loved his wife, too, but their relationship was different. He did not think it was possible to love two women but he did. Emily stole his heart as a child. She was not at all like the other women he knew. She was sweet and kind and it was just easy with her. They could talk for hours without running out of things to say to each other.

The night he met his wife, Bobby, at the party he had expected nothing to come of it. He wanted to take his mind off Emily and it worked until she walked in on them in the bathroom.

His face grew hot at the thought. He hadn't wanted to be Emily's rebound. He wanted to wait until she left Jordan and was ready to be with him.

At first he hung out with Bobby because she took his mind off Emily and she was very sexy. She knew just how to leave him begging for more. Their relationship was exciting, and they had a hard time keeping their hands off each other. They made love in the alley behind their favorite restaurant, and then one crazy night they made love in an abandoned building above an old bar in Duluth.

Bobby liked to smoke when she drank. She had gone outside to have a cigarette with a friend, and when she came back in she was full of energy and falling-over drunk.

"So I was outside with Lisa and we came back in to use the ladies' room, but the line was long so Lisa told me she knew where we could use the bathroom. She brought me out back and into an apartment building above the restaurant. No one lives there anymore and the power is shut off but there's still a lot of the guys' junk up there. I think we should sneak up there and have some fun."

Although the idea was very intriguing to him, he was not drunk enough to consider it a good idea. But instead of saying no, he took a shot of Gray Goose and took her hand as she led him into the abandoned apartment.

"Careful, there's junk all over the floor," she said laughing.

Once his eyes adjusted to the faint light, he could see an outline of Bobby as she led him deeper into the apartment. The streetlight lit the kitchen enough to see a table.

Bobby bent over and knocked everything off it. The junk crashed to the floor. "Hey, someone is going to hear us."

"Oh, come on, don't be such a pansy. The music is so loud downstairs they can't hear a thing, and the other two apartments are abandoned.

Before he could react, she distracted him with her tongue in his mouth. He tried to object, but she was already taking her clothes off. Bobby loved adrenaline rushes and the excitement of doing something that could get her in trouble.

Coming from a rich family, she was always told what to do, and she never got a chance to make her own mistakes. Back in those days he always felt so anxious around her, wondering what idea she would come up with next and whether she would ever settle down. Luckily her thrill-seeking behavior only lasted a few months. Once she started on her PhD, she was a different person. She became responsible, reliable, and content. He almost missed her old behavior because she was so busy with school and did not have much time for him. He was sure she had lost interest in him and the fire was no longer burning between them. One night he brought it up.

"Bobby, do you still love me?"

She closed her computer and stared at him. "Of course I still love you, silly. Why would you say such a thing?" She grabbed his hand and placed it in her lap. "I know I'm really busy right now with school, but it will be over soon." She took a deep breath. "Truth is, there's something I haven't told you. I'm scared you will look at me different."

He squinted at her. What could she do that would make him look at her differently? "You can tell me anything."

She pulled her hand away. She looked so scared. She flipped her long red curls over her shoulder. "Dawson, I'm bipolar. I've known since I was eighteen-years-old. It isn't something I go around telling people. I know sometimes I can be impulsive, but when I take my pills, I can control my highs and lows. It's the reason I went into pharmacy. I wanted to understand more about medicine so I could help others with the same issues and understand what I'm taking and how it affects me."

"Well, that's it, we're over."

Her eyes almost popped out of her head.

He wrapped his arms around her. "I'm just kidding, babe. I love you no matter what. Nothing you can do will scare me off Don't ever be afraid to tell me anything."

"Seriously? That's it?" She sat back against the couch. "I thought you were going to take this so much harder. You do know what bi-polar is, right?"

"Oh babe, I know what bi-polar is, but there's nothing about you that could ever scare me away, although it explains a lot."

She took the pillow off the couch and hit him with it. He tackled her onto the couch. He loosened his grip on her and ran his hand over her shoulder. He kneeled beside the couch "Bobby Jo Lind, I love you with all my heart and soul. I want to be your partner for the rest of our lives and have lots of babies with you. Please say you'll be my wife."

She sat up so fast she knocked heads with him. They both laughed as they held on to their heads. "Yes, yes," she said. "It's about damn time. Now go get me a ring."

He hugged her. Her sarcasm was what made her special. She always shocked him with her one-liners. "Just one thing, do you have any money because I'm broke."

She shook her head and slapped him across the face, leaving him with a stinger. "If I'm paying then I get to pick it out."

. . .

BEFORE DAWSON KNEW IT, it was quarter to eight. He stepped in front of the small mirror in his classroom and adjusted his tie. Bobby would have loved Emily and he was sure she would give him her blessing. She would want him to be happy. He had to back off and remain in the friend zone. She made it clear she wanted to try again with Matthew. He wanted her to find her happiness, even if it was with someone else.

Liz came into his room, a huge smile on her face. "Hey, Dawson. How are you this beautiful morning?"

She never took the hint that he was not interested. "I'm doing alright. Just trying to put together a few things for my class today. How is Franklin this morning?"

"He's okay. This divorce has been so tough on him. I worry about how it will affect him in future, you know?"

Dawson leaned into his desk so she could not get any closer to him. "A lot of kids go through this, he will be just fine. Just take it one day at a time. I'll be the first to tell you if I see any changes in him in the classroom."

"Thank you," she said.

She turned to walk away, but then stopped and turned back around. "So this Emily, you two seem to be kicking it off, huh?"

He was not sure what to say to this. Liz was always so full of drama. "We're old friends and we work together."

"Everyone sees the way you look at her. Just be careful, I think she's bad news."

"Thanks for the heads up. Now I really must finish getting ready for my class."

"Maybe I'll come see you next weekend. I've got this new dark beer, you just have to try it."

"I plan on working all week doing construction, but maybe some other time."

He tried not to be rude, but how could he tell her to leave

without offending her? She was a bully and this was just another way to control him.

"Well, some other time," she said. "Don't be a stranger, I am your neighbor and I don't bite."

He exhaled when she left the room and shook his head. No matter what he said she would never stop trying. Sure she was beautiful and smart, but he never felt any connection with her. Not even before Emily came back into his life.

The bell rang and Anna came in first with Emily following right behind her. He stopped breathing when he saw her and tried to look away but his body would not listen to his mind. How could he have the same reaction every time he saw her? When their eyes met, his heart stopped beating. This was torture but he needed to be strong with respect to her and her family. The last thing he wanted to do was make her feel as uncomfortable as Liz made him feel every day.

CHAPTER 14

Emily

The school year was flying by with just a couple of weeks left before summer break. All the teachers warned her that the last couple of weeks of school were the hardest for the students. They lost their motivation and most teachers took them outside more because it was so hard for them to sit still and learn anything.

Dawson did the same. Minnesota only had a few months of warm weather so he took his class outside for extra recess on sunny days.

Mrs. Eli was teaching Anna to color in the lines, and she helped her focus on her sight words and hand-eye coordination. In Dawson's room, Anna's social skills were improving every day. Emily focused on helping her connect with the other students, but the kids in class knew she was different. No one else had an adult following them around and redirecting them all day. Anna's behaviors gave her away, too.

The girls used baby talk when speaking to her, and they acted more like her mother than her classmate. Likely they were unaware of what they were doing, it just came naturally.

She was reading books on autism to try to better understand Anna's diagnosis and the best ways to work with her. When Anna had horrible behaviors, mainly after a weekend when her schedule changed, Emily would bring her into Mrs. Eli's room and they would listen to light, classical music while they built Legos together. Anna no longer kicked or hit Emily, but she would lay down on the floor and refuse to get up. She would also throw whatever was in her hands and cross her arms and pout.

Mrs. Eli and Emily decided to make a chart with a giant bee. Anna would move the bee when she was good, and when she reached the beehive she could pick a prize front the prize box. The prize box contained some pretty awesome things like necklaces, cards, fidgets, super balls, and even books. Emily worked on coloring the bee chart when Mrs. Eli hogged Anna and pushed her aside. It gave her something to do, and the project was a great stress reliever. She loved to watch her own progress and what she could do when she put in the effort.

Although Mrs. Eli was still quite rude to her, she was much nicer when they were alone. Mrs. Eli still would not let her help when Anna was in her room, but she had come to realize that Mrs. Eli worked better with the kids alone. Once she was done with the bee project, she would sit and color while listening to everything Mrs. Eli did or said to improve her skills working with Anna.

During lunch the teachers shut her out completely so she read a book when Kari was not at lunch. If Kari was there, they sat together in the corner talking. Sometimes they tried to make conversation with the other teachers. They liked to walk around the school to get some exercise. Spring fever was hitting them just like the kids

MEMORIAL WEEKEND CAME and the weather forecast said it was going to be a beautiful and sunny weekend with a high of seventy to seventy-five. Perfect weather for living on a lake. She was finally enjoying lake life, even with all the noise from boats as the weather got warmer and there was no longer any ice on the lake.

The water was still too cold for Irene to swim, but maybe she could work up the courage to jump in at least once by herself.

It was Friday night, and she had just put Irene to bed. It took almost an hour to get her stay in her room. "Mama, I'm thirsty." "Mama, I have to go to the bathroom." She almost lost her temper. "One more book, mama, just one more." She had already read five. She was sick of fighting with her to go to bed. She'd had a long week and she was exhausted. She fell asleep beside Irene that night.

She woke up to a tap, tap, tap. She opened her eyes and froze. What was that noise? She heard it again. Tap, tap, tap, on the door.

Was she still dreaming? Who could be at the door? She sat up and made her way to the noise, careful not to wake Irene. She looked out the window. Dawson was standing there. Her heart dropped.

She opened the door. "Hello."

"I'm sorry, were you sleeping?"

She rubbed her eyes and realized she must look a mess. How late was it? "Not anymore, what's up?"

"I'm sorry I woke you. I was wondering if you would like me to put in your dock tomorrow. I'm putting mine in, and I thought I'd take my boat for a ride after that and maybe show you and Irene the chain of lakes. You haven't been boating through them before, have you?"

How did he have so much energy after a long week of work? She always loved that about him. He was so passionate and excited about most things. "You're going to put the docks in yourself?"

"No, my partner from my construction company is coming to help me. We help each other every year."

"That sounds like a great idea. I'll cook as my gift. Not taking no for an answer," she said before he could object. "Can I ask you a question?"

"Shoot."

"How do you have time to teach and own and work at a construction company anyway?"

"I have a lot of free time and a great partner who pretty much runs it himself. I just listen and do what I'm told. He's the brains of the operation." He turned to go. "See you tomorrow?"

She nodded and he waved goodbye and ran down the driveway.

She closed the door and yawned. If only she had half his energy.

SHE WOKE up to the sun blazing through her window and into her closed eyes. Though a Saturday at five-thirty in the morning, a cup of coffee and the view from her window was enough to get her out of bed with a smile. She slipped on her shoes and stepped outside in a pair of shorts and t-shirt. The air was a little cool, but not enough to chill her.

THE CALM WATER was covered with white pollen. It made the lake look ugly and dirty. That explained why she was so stuffed up this morning. She didn't get allergies until she was an adult, and she only had symptoms a couple times a year. The trees surrounding the lake were reflected on the water. It looked like a painting. She sat and stared at the beautiful scene she was blessed to see every morning from her own porch.

Irene's crying brought her back to reality, and she headed inside to get her. "Hello, sweet girl."

Irene was rubbing her eyes. She crawled on the couch.

"I'll get you some breakfast. How about Rice Crispies?"

They sat at the table, Irene in her big-girl booster seat, and ate their cereal.

She sighed. Matthew was missing all the little changes.

"Guess what? We're going on a boat ride today with mommy's friend."

Irene clapped her hands and smiled. "Yay! Swimming."

"Maybe. Eat up, sweet girl."

They ran into town and spent the morning at Jillian's doing laundry and by the time they got back out to the lake, Dawson was all done and the docks were both in. She put Irene down for a nap and went outside to enjoy the sunshine and pull some weeds.

"And you say I never sit still."

She turned around. Dawson was lounging on his deck in board shorts and no shirt. The muscles on his arms were well defined. His chest had the perfect amount of hair, not too much, and his back was smooth and hairless. She never realized how much he looked like Penn Badgley from *Gossip Girl*. He even had that 'eat your heart out' smirk like him.

"Dawson, hey, you startled me."

"Where's Irene? I'm ready when you are."

"She's taking a nap. I figured you wouldn't enjoy cranky Irene. I like to avoid that when I can."

"You want to jump in the lake while she's sleeping?"

She took a look at the blue water and goosebumps rose on her arms just thinking about it. "How about later? She'll be up soon."

"You promise?"

"Yes."

WHEN IRENE WOKE UP, Emily called Dawson. They put their suits on underneath shorts and a sweatshirt. Layers were the best since the wind could be cold even if it was seventy-five degrees already. She loaded them both up with sunscreen while she waited for him to come out. Irene cried out and moved her head when Emily tried to get her cheeks and forehead.

She stomped her feet and tried to pull away. "No!"

"Just hold still," Emily said.

But Irene was not listening. She walked away.

"Irene you have a white face, let me rub it in."

Dawson joined them, a cooler in one hand and towels in the other. "You're listening to you mommy, aren't you, Irene?"

Irene nodded, no longer defiant as she walked back to her mom, still staring at Dawson.

Emily smoothed the sunscreen in. "All done. Let's go boating."

Dawson got into the boat first and lifted Irene in.

Irene jumped up and down. "Me drive?"

"You bet! You can be my co-captain.

He placed one of his red and white baseball caps on her head, then started the boat and slowly backed up. He made his way under the bridge and through the channel to West Sturgeon.

Emily relaxed and enjoyed the view. The coast was lined

with beautiful cabins and homes that were as big as Dawson's or even bigger.

"Do a lot of people live out here?" she said over the loud motor.

He turned his head. "Yeah many do, but others have second homes or cabins out here and just stay for the summer. This is the best time of year to see the homes because the trees are bare so they don't block our view of the houses. They're stunning, million-dollar homes."

"I can see that," she said.

She sat back and let her hair blow in the wind as she watched the water and the houses. She waved at other boats and pontoons as they went by. Everyone was so friendly. Irene was grinning ear to ear as she held onto the wheel. Dawson held the wheel from the bottom so Irene felt like she was really steering. Every now and then Dawson said something in Irene's ear, and she would get really excited and point and scream.

Florida was beautiful, the Gulf was beautiful, but nothing beat this view. They could stop the boat in the middle of the lake and jump in without worries of what was in the water. She understood why so many people wanted to be on the chain and every person they passed smiled. Some cabins had water trampolines and even water slides going into the lake. Too bad Jillian's boat did not work, but Gabby said it hadn't worked in years.

They stopped at McCarthy Beach on Side Lake, and Dawson laid out a big blanket for them to sit on the beach. He opened his cooler and handed out bottles of water to her and Irene and one for himself. He gave them each peanut butter and jelly sandwiches. He also brought chips and double-stuffed Oreos, her favorite.

She laughed at the sandwiches. Dawson knew they liked

peanut butter and jelly because she mentioned it at school one day. She loved that he remembered.

Irene ate a couple bites of her sandwich and then she took off her pants and walked into the water, ankle deep. Finally.

"Brr," she said.

Emily and Dawson laughed at the look on her face, like she had just taken a big bite out of a lemon.

Another family was on the beach. A little girl about three years older than Irene came over and they built a sand castle together.

"This is one of the shallowest lakes. You and I could walk out to those buoys way out there and still be able to touch the bottom," Dawson said.

"Really? I can hardly even see that far."

"Yes, it's shallow."

"That's crazy. Well, thank you so much for taking us out today, we needed this. Irene has been missing her dad and the transition has been so hard. I have a hard time getting her to sleep at night. Sometimes I fall asleep trying to get her down."

"Any time. I plan on boating a lot this summer, and it's nice to have company. Remember all those days at the beach growing up? Building sandcastles and watching you get blisters on your shoulders because you hated putting on sunscreen."

Memories of the day at the ocean when she could not go in the sun because of her burns and Dawson made castles with Lindsey instead came flooding in. She pushed the thoughts from her mind.

"What's wrong?"

"Nothing. It's just that ever since I moved here I always thought I'd eventually move back to Florida. I hate the cold, and I miss the ocean, but after today I realize how beautiful

Minnesota is. And I can't believe I'm sitting here with you after all these years, Dawson."

"Ditto," he said and laughed. "You really love him don't you?"

"Who? Matthew?"

Dawson nodded, taking a sip of his water.

Did she love him? She was not so sure anymore. "He may be my ex-husband, but he is Irene's father. If there is any chance we can make it work, I have to know I tried my best."

IRENE'S NEW FRIEND LEFT, but the sand castle was only half done.

"Hey, I like building sand castles," Dawson said. He leaned over. "Let's get mommy to help us, too.

They worked together to make it three feet high and a dug a stream around it.

She sat back. "I have to admit, it's probably the best sand castle I have ever built."

It had been years since she made a sand castle. She took a picture of Irene and Dawson standing next to it with her phone. Irene had her arm around his neck and he was kneeling beside her. It warmed her heart that Irene was so taken with Dawson.

He gave them both high fives. "That is one heck of a castle."

"Can we take it home, mommy?"

"I don't think it will hold up very well in the boat. Let's leave it here for some other little girl or boy to see."

Her lip slipped into a pout. "Okay."

"Are you ready to drive the boat again, captain?" Dawson said.

"Yeah!" She ran for the boat and splashed into the water.

Emily was so relaxed, she fell asleep in the boat. She woke

up when Dawson quieted the motor and glided to the dock. It was almost eight-thirty, and the sun was beginning to set in the sky.

He tied off the boat and helped Emily out and then lifted Irene high above his head and out of the boat. She squealed. "I'm going to put Irene to bed and then would you like to sit out by the lake and have a glass of wine with me? It's the least I can do after everything you've done for us today. I wish I had time to cook you dinner. I had no idea we'd be out this late."

"Don't worry about it, wine sounds perfect."

SHE PUT Irene to bed and for the first time, Irene fell asleep just two pages into the book without a fuss. The fresh air must have done its magic.

She jumped in the shower and changed her clothes, and put on a little mascara. Dawson was already sitting on the beach with a towel underneath him. She handed him the monitor and a wine glass, then poured them glasses of chardonnay.

"Cheers," she said, clinking glasses with him.

They watched the sun's final descent.

She leaned back in the sand and sighed. "I never expected being a PSA would be so difficult."

"You do an amazing job. You truly make it look easy."

"Really?"

She thought about all the days she struggled with getting Anna to listen. She was truly grateful for the team of helpers she had to call on when she ran out of ideas. Even Mrs. Eli, she hated to admit.

"Yes really. But what's up with you and those teachers? I've noticed a little friction in the air."

Dawson always seemed so clueless. How odd that he saw

the friction. "I'm not a fan of Mrs. Eli or maybe she isn't a fan of mine."

"Liz, or Mrs. Eli as you call her, is kind of a know-it-all, but not without good reason. She really does know what she's doing."

"You're taking her side? You have no idea what I deal with every day. She's good with Anna, but she doesn't teach me a thing. She wants a pat on the back all the time. I have to watch her to get any ideas at all. She almost puts me in a timeout until it's time for me to take Anna back to class. It's weird."

Dawson played with the sand, and avoided making eye contact. "I'm not a big fan of hers myself, but she's been through a lot. Her cabin is just two over from me. I've heard her and her husband go at it. She's that way for a reason. He's now her ex-husband, but she doesn't want anyone to think she failed at something so she hides the hurt."

He was standing up for her arch nemesis, but that showed how caring he was. Especially if he admitted to not liking her either. Did he not realize everyone knew Mrs. Eli had the hots for him? He needed to open his eyes. He couldn't be that blind. He knew. He had to.

He stood up and drank the last of the wine in his glass.

Was he going to call it a night?

Instead, he took off his shirt. "Don't forget you made me a promise."

She turned away before he could see the lust in her eyes, and poured another glass of wine. "Sorry, I didn't bring my suit."

"Oh, you aren't getting out of it that easy. You promised me."

He bent down and pulled on her bra strap and made it snap. "You do have a bra and underwear on. It covers all the same things."

She groaned. "Fine. You got me."

She stood up and pulled down her pants. She turned her back to him as she took off her shirt, but his eyes were on her, and she loved it. Thank goodness she took the time to shave and she was wearing a matching set of bra and underwear. She had always been thin, but her stomach was not flat, and she had light stretch marks by her belly button that made her insecure. "Catch me if you can."

She raced full speed into the lake, stubbed her toe, and fell into the water.

Dawson ran after her and patted her on the back as she coughed and fought to catch her breath.

"Are you okay?"

She coughed once more and nodded. "I'm still a klutz. Do you remember when you taught me to do the butterfly in your pool that summer?"

"Do I ever. You looked like a drowning rat. You were weak."

She splashed him in the face, and he reached out and grabbed her. He held her close and then threw her into the water. When she stood up her bra straps were down on her arms. He moved in and pulled them both up for her like a gentleman. She wrapped her hands around his neck and stared into his eyes.

They both leaned in, and he kissed her. His lips were soft but sweet like the water or maybe she was tasting the wine.

She should pull away, but she stayed and enjoyed his sweet mouth. Sparks flew between them, but the ring on her finger brought her back to reality. She pulled away. She may not be married, but she wasn't exactly on the market yet either.

He leaned in for more but she put her arm out to stop him. "I'm sorry, but I just can't."

He touched her arm. "Okay, but please don't go."

She was inches from his face. She rested her forehead against him. "Why do we always have such terrible timing?"

Her heart ached to touch his lips again. She took her finger and ran it across his lips before he could say anything. "You're my drug, Dawson. I just can't get enough of you."

"Every day I spend with you is torture because I know you can't be with me. I screwed up all those years ago. I ran away when I should have been walking away with you."

She had a hard time meeting his eyes. If she did, she would be unable to control her urge for more. "But then you wouldn't have met Bobby."

"I have no regrets marrying my wife, Em. After I lost her, I thought I would never be able to love again, and then I saw you that night on the road and I knew it was you right away but I was afraid to say anything. You made me remember what it is like to love again. I really hope Matthew appreciates what he has with you because you deserve the best."

She pulled away from him. "I have to go, Dawson, before you say anymore. I had a wonderful evening, but this can't happen again, okay? I'm sorry, but I don't like you like that anymore. I was caught up in the moment."

The sparkle left his eyes and his face was somber.

"Goodnight, Dawson."

She walked away from him and picked up her clothes from the sand. She pulled her underwear up and slipped her shirt over her head. She felt his eyes on her, and it killed her not to look back at him. She may not technically be married, but Matthew was still her husband in her mind. She wanted to make it work when he got out, or she would never forgive herself.

CHAPTER 15

$\mathcal{T}$he last week of school before summer vacation the students were bouncing with energy. The teachers expected this so the last week was all about social skills and having fun. Tuesday was fun day and Emily could not wait for Anna to see the gigantic bouncy houses outside, and all the outdoor games set up. They had popcorn, snow cones, and cotton candy stalls. She tried talking to Anna about the day, but the little girl did not understand what was going on.

At ten o'clock, Dawson's class got to enjoy the fun day for a whole hour. Like expected, as soon as Anna saw the bouncy house she jumped up and down and ran inside. She climbed through the house and jumped for a long time. There were only two kindergarten classes so they let Anna stay in for almost the whole hour. When she finally got out she wanted a snow cone.

Emily pulled Anna's messy hair into a ponytail while they waited in line.

"Hello."

Emily turned around and almost lost the hold she had on

Anna's hair because they both turned so fast at the voice behind them.

"Mommy," Anna said and hugged the woman.

"You must be Miss Emily. I've heard so much about you."

Anna's mom was dressed in a fancy red shirt and black shorts. Her hair was pulled back into a French braid. She held out her hand. "It is so nice to meet you, Mrs.?"

Anna grabbed a blue snow cone, took one bite and threw it away. "Can I go back in the bouncy house?"

Emily nodded.

Anna's mom's eyes were kind and loving as she watched Anna run away.

They walked together in the direction of the bouncy house.

"I'm Lynn and I am so glad to meet the teacher behind Anna's transformation this year."

She smiled. "Thank you, I don't know if that's all true."

"No, really. She listens better, she wants to read books with me all the time, and she seems ... happier. Will you please share your secret?"

How should she answer Anna's mother? Anna was behaving better, but she was a long way from being fully responsible. "Anna is a wonderful little girl, but her good home life helps, too. We have a great team here. Mrs. Eli has shown me so much, and she is magical with Anna. She's even taught me patience," she said. That was not really a lie. She observed and learned from Mrs. Eli. "She is really the person you need to thank."

"You are very humble. I don't know what she's going to do all summer without you. I'm not sure if Mrs. Eli told you, but Anna's last day is tomorrow because we are leaving for Hawaii on Thursday for two weeks."

" No, she didn't say anything to me, but that sounds really exciting."

"Can I get your advice on something? I'm a little nervous flying with Anna because of her meltdowns. I know she's been doing much better, but we both know that losing her normal structure and routine may set her off. People get angry when her behaviors start, and going through security is the worst. They judge me and give me horrible looks." She shuddered. "It's so frustrating. Do you have any advice? You know how challenging her behaviors can be."

Trying to get a hostile Anna through airport security was unimaginable. Security was exhausting for her, and she was an adult. She had an idea. "Why don't you get a wheel chair for her? People understand physical needs better than things they can't see. That way if she does have behaviors, they will think it's because of something physically wrong. Also they usually let you move to the front of the security line."

Lynn hugged her. "You're a genius. Thank you so much. I think you just saved me a lot of stress."

Dawson came over and blew his whistle. "Time to line up kids."

"Good-by Lynn, and have a great vacation."

"That was really good advice you gave her," Dawson said. "I never would have thought of that. You just saved that family a lot of frustration and exhaustion."

IN THE TEACHER'S LOUNGE, Kari was running late so Emily sat down in her favorite corner.

"Is it true that your husband is in prison?" Jan said. The other teachers laughed.

"I really don't see why that is any of your business," Emily said. "Do you feel better now that you got that out there? Did you think you were going to embarrass me? Because you're the one that looks like a jerk right now for asking that."

Jan stopped chewing and her face reddened. She turned

her head to talk with Addie and Ellen as if this conversation never happened.

Kari stood in the doorway and gave her a thumbs up. "Want to have lunch outside?"

Once they were outside Kari started laughing. "Wow, you sure put her in her place."

"I don't understand what her problem is. I did nothing to her. I'm so sick of the way she treats people."

Kari put a grape in her mouth. "She's a mean girl. She thinks she's being blunt, but she's a horrible person. That was awesome. You seriously made my day."

Mrs. Eli and Jan made the rest of Emily's day uncomfortable. They gave her evil looks in the hallway every time she passed them, which was awkward since they were all walking their classes down the hallway. When Anna and Emily walked past Jan's room, Anna was talking loudly. She tried to quiet her down then Jan came stomping over. "Now that's just rude. At least by now you should be capable of controlling your student."

She was in no mood to argue with Jan. "I'm sorry."

They were purposely going out of their way to hurt her after her one comment to Jan. She went to the bathroom and when she came out Mrs. Eli was talking to Dawson and pointing at her. She turned her back to them and picked up a book to read to the kids. By the time she was done, Mrs. Eli was gone and Dawson waved her over and told the children to sit in their desks.

"Hey, I'm not sure what happened between you and Mrs. Johnson, but the principal wants to see you in her office."

She groaned. They were all ganging up on her. She walked in and the secretary told her to have a seat without a smile. Was everyone a Mrs. Eli minion? Did they not have a mind of their own?

Mrs. Voughn opened up her door a couple minutes later

and told her to come in. "I asked you to meet with me because I was addressed with some concerns about your behavior and supervision."

She did not understand. She did a very good job with Anna and never let her out of her sight. No matter how bad Mrs. Eli got she never talked back. She did her job and went home. "Supervision?"

"I have had multiple reports from multiple sources that you aren't watching your student, and you don't try to control her behaviors. You let your student scream outside a teacher's classroom and didn't even try to calm her down. I was told you have a horrible attitude and bully some of the other teachers."

Bully! Ha! She could not believe what she was hearing. She was a bully? This was so far from the truth and Mrs. Voughn knew it. She stood up for herself for the first time today and this is what she got?

"I can promise you, I have never bullied a person in my life. I can tell you that I am not the problem. Have you asked Dawson, my other supervisor?"

Mrs. Voughn eyed her suspiciously. "You call him Dawson, huh? We ask that you're respectful of all teachers here and you don't address them in this school by their first name, only by their last. We have some really great teachers here and I ask all my PSA's to make sure to help the teachers in any way they can. These teachers shape the children for their future and you are there to help by making the class-room easier for them. Do you understand this?"

She was told on the first day to call all the teachers by their first name. She knew this was a set-up. Was she implying that teachers are more important than PSA's and not to piss them off or she would lose her job? Was this really happening? What a load of crap.

"Yes," she said.

"If you continue to have a relationship with Mr. Kersich, and it gets in the way of the classroom or makes other teachers feel uncomfortable, I will have to let you go. Do you understand?"

"Yes," she said again.

The principal was warning her that if she did not bow down to the teachers she would be let go and since she was being warned, the firing would be justified. This was a load of crap.

What she really wanted to do was tell her the truth, but the truth did not matter. This was very one-sided, and she did not matter.

WHEN THE LONG school day was finally over, Emily could not wait to get to Jillian's to see Irene. Her daughter had a way of always making her feel better, even on her worst days. The big smiles and tight hugs were the best way to make her heart heal.

"Do you mind if she stays the night with me?" Jillian said. "There's story time at the library at six tonight and Gabby is going to read her book to the kids. You're more than welcome to come but you look exhausted and I thought you could use a nap."

"That would be fine. Yeah, I had a horrible day, and I'd rather not tonight."

She wanted to take Irene home and snuggle with her, but that was selfish. Irene loved the library and she did not want to get in the way of that.

She was back at the cabin by six after stopping to get some groceries on her way. Dawson was outside grilling, and he waved. Her hands were full so she did not have to wave back. He closed the grill and came running over to help her carry in groceries.

She grabbed a bag. "You don't need to help."

"I don't mind, I just turned on the grill. Where's Irene?"

"She's staying at Jillian's tonight."

He juggled the bags in one arm and jumped ahead to open the door. "Well, since it's just you, I have two T-bones marinating, would you like to have dinner with me?"

"I don't know, I have a pounding headache and I'm exhausted. Maybe another night?"

"Oh Emily, I know you better than that. What's wrong? What happened with Mrs. Voughn?"

He wouldn't understand. She put the last two bags on the counter and started putting groceries in the fridge. "It's nothing, really."

He put the yogurts she had in her hand back into the bag. "What happened?"

She needed to vent and it all came pouring out. "It's your stupid friend Mrs. Eli and Mrs. Johnson. They told Mrs. Voughn I'm a bully."

He started laughing.

Fine. She continued putting groceries away.

"I'm sorry, I don't mean to laugh but everyone knows you're no bully. Don't listen to them."

"The principal listened to them." She whipped open the fridge. "It's all because Mrs. Eli has a crush on you, you know."

"Oh, stop. She's just upset because we're friends."

"Do you know what Mrs. Voughn said when I accidentally called you Dawson? That I can't call you by your first name, and teachers are way more important than I am so I can't piss them off or I'm fired."

Dawson handed her more groceries to put in the fridge. "She did not say that."

"I'm serious. I don't matter to them. They think I'm just

135

easily replaceable. Do you know how many people want my job? It's the perfect job for moms. She threatened me."

"I won't let that happen, okay? I'll talk to her next week. Let me make you a steak tonight. Think about it, you won't have to cook and they're delicious. I've been marinating them all day while you were bullying the teachers."

Emily threw the bread at him. He caught it and laughed. "Oh, I'm just kidding. I'll stop teasing you if you say yes."

"Fine!"

HE KEPT HIS WORD. They ate their dinner on her dock at her request so they could watch as the boats cruised by and take in the peaceful scenery.

She popped a piece of steak in her mouth. "You really are an amazing cook, you know that."

"Thank you. My wife would sit on the dock for hours and watch the boats go by. She'd speak to her belly and tell our baby a play-by-play of the beach, the birds, and about life. She'd talk about the lakes and the sunshine and the people here. We were only at Side Lake a couple of months when she told me there were no people in this world like the Side-lakers. They had their own little community and took care of one another, but yet left each other alone to enjoy nature, too. Some gossip floated around but everyone went out of their way to welcome a newcomer."

"It sounds much better than Hibbing," she said.

"Just different. It is smaller so they all know each other by having running and skiing groups, groups that walk around the lakes, and a bunch of other stuff. "

"Do they do anything for kids?"

"The rec center puts on a bunch of stuff for the kids throughout the summer like a camp slash daycare. My favorite is men even have weekly Smear tournaments at the two restaurants here. It's really cool."

She loved the way his face lit up when he talked about Side Lake. She understood why he and his wife wanted to move here and start a family. Her heart broke for him.

He put his hand on hers as they watched the sun go down. "I know the kiss really upset you, but I haven't felt this way about anyone since, well my wife was alive. Bobby knew about you, by the way. She understood you would always be a part of my life. She accepted me and all my flaws. You really would have liked her. "

"Knew about me? What do you mean?"

"Oh, Emily, I never stopped loving you, you know that."

She wasn't sure what to say. "I still can't believe she was the woman I caught you with in the bathroom that night. I will never forget it. Your pants were around your ankles and her face popped out." She shivered at the thought.

"It's kind of funny if you think about it. I never thought it would become what it did with her. I just knew you were off limits, and I needed to step away somehow. For what it's worth, I wanted to be with you more than anything that night."

She did not want to think about that night anymore. "I can't believe Jan had the nerve to mention Matthew being in prison in front of everyone."

"She did?"

"Of course she did. You don't know how evil those girls are, Dawson. And I just found out Matthew got in trouble for making booze or something in prison and his time is extended until June. I really thought he was going to change this time."

"What's going to happen when he gets out of prison?"

"I have to try to make it work. I told you that. He needs me."

"Do you love him?"

"Of course, I love him. If it were Bobby, would you give her another try?"

The pain on his face threw her. She had gone too far.

"That isn't fair," he said.

"I know, I'm sorry. I didn't mean for it to come out like that."

"I know."

"Dawson!" A woman called from behind them, but she could not tell who it was.

"Oh crap," Dawson said. "I'm so sorry."

Oh no.

"You did say to come over for a fire tonight, right? Then I said, it's a date and we laughed, remember?" Liz said.

She looked behind Dawson and pretended not to see Emily, but she knew better.

"Oh is that you, Emily? I didn't see you there. I did hear you moved into this tiny little hole in the wall next to Dawson. It's ... nice."

"Be nice, Liz," he said.

She laughed and gently pushed on Dawson's chest. She dragged her fingertips all the way to his bicep and then squeezed it and laughed, batting her eyelashes. "I'm always nice. You sure have some big muscles, Dawson, doesn't he, Emily?"

He pulled his arm away. "Enough."

"What? I'm just teasing," she said.

"You two have your fun, I'm going to bed," Emily said. Anything to leave this uncomfortable conversation and get away from Liz.

"Don't go, the fire is just starting," Dawson said.

"Sorry, I'm exhausted. Have fun, nice seeing you, Mrs. Eli," she said through clenched teeth.

"I'll walk you," Dawson said, taking a step in her direction.

She waved him off. "No, no, it's fine. I'm just right here. Have fun."

She could not wait to get into her house and shut the door. Why would Dawson invite Mrs. Eli over? If he wanted Mrs. Eli he could have her.

CHAPTER 16

Emily

The next day was another beautiful, sunny day in May. It was way too nice to be stuck indoors. Anna was having a great day, which kept them out of Mrs. Eli's room, and she was grateful for that. She had to be in Dawson's class all day, but luckily he was so busy he did not have a chance to talk to her about the previous night.

Mrs. Voughn came into Dawson's room and talked to him near the end of the day.

"Emily, can you come to my office?"

She followed Mrs. Voughn down the hallway, not a word exchanged between them until Mrs. Voughn shut her office door.

"Two times in two days. I can only assume this isn't a good visit," Emily said.

She would not play games with them anymore or put up with being told teachers' jobs were more important than hers. Teachers would go crazy if they did not have PSA's to help.

"I wish I could say you're wrong."

Here we go. "I've been in class all day. I did not go to the teachers' lounge today because of the conversation we had yesterday. I'm trying to avoid this continued problem so I really don't know what teachers could be complaining about now."

"Calm down, Mrs. Fredrickson."

Mrs. Voughn was calling her by her last name again just to be rude.

"No one said you were harassing them today, but I do have reason to believe you did not take our talk yesterday very seriously."

What was she referring to? Had to be more lies, just to get her fired. "What do you mean?"

"Like I told you already, we expect you to be a good role model and you seem to be getting quite comfortable with Mr. Kersich after hours."

"He's my neighbor. We've known each other since we were children. I really don't understand why that has anything to do with my job here."

"Well, there are pictures circulating, and it is making the other teachers feel uncomfortable."

"Pictures? I don't know about any pictures. What are they pictures of?"

"Oh I think we both know what they are of. This may be turning into an HR issue so I better not say."

She acted like she had sex tapes of them or something. She was fishing for a confession or to get Emily to say she would stop being friends with Dawson. Would Mrs. Eli stoop so low to make this up?

"Why do I have the feeling this came from Mrs. Eli? I can assure you there are no pictures. Did Mrs. Eli tell you she

141

came over to Dawson's house for beers? She probably made this up because I was there with him when she arrived. Why isn't that a problem? Because they're teachers? Why it is a problem if a PSA is around a teacher outside of school floors me. If there are any pictures circulating it is because Mrs. Eli was spying on us. "

"That is quite an assumption, dear. I think I've made myself clear about the way I feel," Mrs. Voughn said.

She stood up. This had gone too far and she would no longer keep quiet. "Excuse me, but one of your teachers has a crush on my best friend, and she's harassing us because we're friends outside of work. Maybe she is the one you need to have a conversation with. My husband and I are divorced, not that it is any of your business. What you are doing here is illegal, and I'm not afraid to press charges on you for harassment. A teacher is no more important than me, but if you feel this way I don't want to work for you any longer. Maybe the superintendent should be alerted to what is going on in this school, don't you think? I'll finish out the day because that is best for Anna. She's going away tomorrow, so this is her last day of school anyway and then I resign. How does that sound?"

Mrs. Voughn shifted in her chair and paled when she mentioned a lawsuit and speaking to the superintendent. Maybe she could talk to Travis about getting his dad to threaten her a little bit. She loved her job, but she was not going to put up with this crap anymore. She had the summer to find a new profession.

She put on a tough front in the principal's office, but the minute she reached the bathroom, she collapsed in tears. How she was going to pull herself together for the last hour of the day? She needed to do it for Anna. She splashed water on her face, looked in the mirror and said, "You are strong enough, you are kind enough, you can overcome your fear.

Do it for Anna." She posed like a superhero with her hands on her hips and her chin held high for close to two minutes. She put a smile on her face and returned to Anna's side feeling much lighter.

She rolled up Anna's school artwork and pulled everything out of her cubby that had been on the walls in the classroom or by the library. She took Anna's name tag off her desk and put it in her backpack. "Say good-bye to everyone, Anna."

Anna hugged her classmates. Even the students who did not want a hug, like the boys, but they had no choice. On the way out the door, Anna blew them all kisses. The kids were too busy packing up their cubbies to notice, but Anna did not care. She skipped down the hallway and Emily followed. It may be against the rules to skip in the school, but so what. This was Anna's last day and sadly, her last day, too. Two jobs in a couple of months. She was on a roll.

She played paper, rocks, and scissors with Anna until her van arrived, and then she walked her out and buckled her up. "Goodbye, Anna. I'm going to miss you."

"Love you, Miss Emily," Anna said and gave her a big hug.

Emily watched the van until it was out of sight. She felt like Anna was her own child and she would never see her again. They had such a bond and although she felt some relief because it did get exhausting keeping up with Anna and constantly redirecting her, she was also heart broken. She wanted to come back next year and be with Anna. This job made her feel better as a person, and Anna made her want to be a better person. Who knew Anna would change her so much?

She walked around the school instead of through the school to avoid everyone, including Dawson. She unlocked her car but stopped at a voice behind her.

"Hey, girl, one more day," Kari said.

"Not for me, I'm done as of today."

"What happened? What do you mean?"

"I kind of quit."

"Quit?"

"Yeah, the teachers made up a bunch of lies about me. Mrs. Voughn threatened me, and told me I needed to please the teachers. She said teachers were complaining about my relationship with Dawson but funny how he was not called to the principal's office, nor were the other teachers. To sum it up, I threatened to go to the superintendent or sue, and then I told her I was quitting."

"Oh no. Wait a minute, Mr. K was going into Mrs. Voughn's office when I left and she did not seem happy. I bet he's in trouble, too."

"Whatever, he's a teacher so he's incapable of doing something wrong. Mrs. Eli even gave the principal pictures of Dawson and me but I never took any pictures so I'm pretty sure she's been stalking us."

"Wow, she really does have it out for you, doesn't she? Well, you'll never have to see her again."

Emily laughed. "Except she has a cabin just a couple doors down from mine."

Her phone vibrated.

"Who is it?" Kari said.

"Dawson."

"You should answer it."

"No. I really don't want to hear what he has to say. I'm just so angry." She put the phone in her pocket. "Let's get together this summer though. I don't know how I would have survived this school year without you, and I'm sorry we won't be working together next year."

"Definitely," Kari said. "I'm really going to miss you, too. And Emily, call Dawson back. This isn't his fault, he's only guilty of being an oblivious man."

. . .

JILLIAN STOOD on the front step while Irene ran though the sprinkler. "Such a beautiful day," she said as Emily walked up the driveway.

"Mommy!" Irene ran up to give Emily a big, wet hug.

"Hey sweet girl, you think it's funny getting mommy all wet?"

She nodded and then ran back to the sprinklers. "Mommy, watch me, watch me."

She sat down at the picnic table and watched while Irene ran though the sprinkler as fast as she could. She was laughing as if she did not know she was going to get wet. How lucky children were to be so innocent. She would be three in a couple months already. Time was flying by. Before she knew it, Irene would be a teenager who wanted nothing to do with her.

She jumped up and ran through the sprinkler with Irene again and again. She was soaking wet and it felt good not to care. Being an adult should not be so serious all the time. It should include more jumping through mud puddles and getting her hair wet. She wiped her face with a towel and sat next to Jillian at the picnic table.

"I think Irene and I are going to stay at Matthew's place tonight. Do you know when he's getting out? Have you talked to him lately?"

"Within the next couple of days he said. Why are you staying there when it is so beautiful at the cabin? Don't you like it there anymore?" Jillian said.

"No, it's beautiful. It's just that my neighbor is my boss, and I'm kind of trying to avoid him right now. It's hard to distance myself from him when he's right next door, you know."

"Sounds like this teacher may mean a little more to you than you're letting on."

"Jillian," she said in a deep voice.

She blinked her eyes, all innocent. "What? I'm just saying you're a single woman now. It's okay to have feelings for someone else. What are you so scared of?"

"I'm not giving up on Matthew, I just can't. And I don't have feelings for Dawson. I don't."

"Mmm hmm."

CHAPTER 17

Matthew

*H*e walked in the front door. The house was much emptier than when he left. Most of Emily's stuff was gone. One side of their walk-in closet was empty except for a few things, including her wedding dress.

He lifted it from the plastic and smelled it. It smelled like Emily, a mixture of strawberry and soap that would never fade from his memory. He pulled a box from the back of the closet. Inside was a lock of brown hair, and a picture of a little baby girl. The color was starting to fade. He put the lock of hair and picture back in the box and pushed the box to the back of the closet. Why would Emily hold onto a lock of hair? Whose was it?

THE SHOWER WAS much warmer and stronger than the prison shower. Oh, how he missed the water pressure and privacy.

Would Emily be glad to see him and smile? Or would she scream at him?

When the shower finally turned cold, he dried off and secured the towel around his waist. He opened the bathroom door and heard a bang. It took him a minute to realize he had hit someone with the door. He pulled the door back and looked around it. Emily was on the floor, holding her head and squeezing her eyes.

"I'm so sorry," he said.

He bent down to help her up. She grabbed on and stood up, but then his towel dropped. Emily looked behind her. Irene must be in the other room. He pulled up his towel, but Emily shielded her eyes. She would not even look at him.

"What the heck are you doing back already? When did you get in? You scared the crap out of me," she said.

Even though they had not seen each other for so long, she did not seem pleased to see him.

"I got out early and I wanted to surprise everyone so I took a cab. It's great to see you, too. I'm going to put some pants on quick. Is Irene in the living room?"

She nodded.

"I'll be right back."

He shut the bedroom door, the room he had shared with her for so many years. He dropped the towel and stared at himself in the mirror. He had gained so much muscle. Had she even noticed? He was overthinking it. She had to still love him. She would never move on that fast. He got dressed and when he opened the door Irene was waiting for him with a big hug.

"Daddy, you're home!" She screamed. "Mommy, daddy's home!"

She had grown so much since he left. How much had he missed out on?

"We were just leaving, but we can stay a little bit, "Emily said.

"Jillian agreed to stay with me for a while. I was hoping Irene could maybe stay the night. I've missed her so much."

He wanted her to stay, too. Why had he sent her divorce papers?

Irene was playing on the floor with toys she had left behind.

"Daddy, play with me," she said.

"One second sweetheart." He turned back to Emily, talking in a whisper. "I've missed you, and I'm really sorry about the divorce papers. Will you stick around and maybe we can talk after Irene goes to sleep? Jillian won't be coming for a few hours. I told her I'd call her after you left."

She looked at her watch, then back at him. "Okay."

He read Irene a couple books and then it was Emily's turn so he went downstairs. Jillian arrived.

He hugged her. She was like a mother to him and he loved her dearly, but he was going to get sick of her bossing him around.

"So how are you doing?" she said. "You seem to be in a good mood."

"I am," he said. "You're early. I hope you aren't trying to interfere with me and Emily again."

"Don't worry, I plan on going to bed but I do want to say one thing."

He gritted his teeth. "What?"

She touched his hand, and he pulled away. "I love you like a son, and I love Emily, too. Just promise me you will really think this through. You and Emily just don't work together. You created a beautiful little girl together, but you need to let her move on now."

"Thanks for the pep talk, Auntie. I guess it's up to Emily, isn't it?"

"I just want what's best for you. It's your life. You're going to do what you think is best in the end and I support you, but I have to tell you what I think."

"I have to fight for her this time. Show her I've changed." He really meant this. He had to give it another shot.

"I really hope so. I don't want this to get messy. I told you both what I think, but ultimately it's your decision, I guess."

She hugged him. "Good night."

Emily came downstairs and sat down beside him on the couch, stiff and robot-like. She did not look at him.

Matthew touched her chin and lifted it. "I know it was rude of me to serve you divorce papers without talking to you. I want you to know I regret what I did. I got some bad advice."

She nodded.

"Are you really not talking to me? I said I'm sorry."

It was just like Emily to act this way. He already told her he was sorry, but he was not going to beg for her forgiveness.

"A lot has happened this past year, Matthew. I really want to trust you again, it's just going to take a while."

"You can't hold onto the past. I'm a different person now. I've been through treatment and I went to prison for my mistakes. I've had a long time out, and I've paid my dues. You need to stop punishing me.

"I'm sorry, I'll try."

"Stay the night with me, make love to me," he said. How long had it been?

She moved away from him on the couch. "Matthew, you filed for divorce, I signed the papers. We are divorced now. Do you just want to pretend that didn't happen?"

"I'm so sorry. I thought I was doing the right thing by

letting you go, but now seeing you, I was wrong. I want our family back together. I want to be with you."

He put his hand on her cheek and moved in for a kiss.

She stood up before he made contact. " I want to try, too, but not this way. No kissing and no intimacy until we both feel it's right, okay? I need time to think. Let's take it slow."

He sighed and leaned his head on the couch back. She had no idea what he went through in prison. They had been together for years, how did she expect him to slow down? What did she want? Did she want him to pretend they just started dating again? Because if he wanted a new relationship it would not be with her. They did this already. The silence grew uncomfortable and he had no idea what he was supposed to say. "So, how has Irene been?"

"She's okay. Missed her dad as you can see."

He wished everything could just go back to what it was like before all of this happened. Forget it all and just move forward. "I'm sorry. In my defense it wasn't on purpose."

"Really? You're going there? What, did someone hold you down and make you smoke meth at our daughter's birthday party? I've been raising her all by myself though it wasn't any different when you were around."

"Then why are you here? If you didn't know I was coming home, why were you in MY house then?"

They both looked down at the phone vibrating on the table. Dawson Home.

She grabbed her phone off the table and threw it in her purse.

"Who is Dawson?"

"A friend," she said.

"This isn't Dawson Dawson? Is it?"

She turned around and he stepped in front of her. "You don't love me anymore, do you?"

"Do you love me?" she asked.

All those days in prison when he lay in bed thinking about the way it would be were a fantasy, not a reality.

"Yes, but to be fair, you didn't even notice or seem to care that I wasn't around. Did you even know I was using? Our relationship was already over."

"Truth is, I've asked myself that over and over. We used to be so close, what happened?"

A fire was burning in the pit of his stomach. "I don't know. Do you even care about me at all anymore? Did you think about me while I was gone?"

She uncrossed her arms and put her hand on his arm. "All I thought about while you were gone was that I wanted to help you. Since the day I met you I wanted to help you, but maybe that was because I never got to help my mom and I don't want anything to happen to you."

"Emily, it won't. I won't ruin my life again. I don't ever want to go back to prison or jeopardize my time with Irene." He smiled. "It's hard, but at least we don't have to go through a divorce again. Maybe it can be different between us now. Let's see if things have changed now that I'm sober. I miss the way we used to be, and I don't want to let you go until we know for sure."

She smiled and hugged him. "A fresh start. I love you, Matthew, but I can't promise I'll get over what you did anytime soon. You put our lives in jeopardy. I could have lost everything."

"I know, I felt it too. I really am sorry for all the pain I've caused."

"I'm really glad we feel the same way," she said, planting a gentle kiss on his forehead. "And I'm so glad you're out of there."

"Me too."

"I get the bed tonight."

"Fine. The couch is like the Hilton for me anyway after being in prison and sleeping on that uncomfortable mattress for months." He punched the couch pillow. "Goodnight, my sweet Emily."

"Goodnight."

CHAPTER 18

Dawson

The last day of school was on the last day of May. The kids were obnoxious and ignored everything he said. No teaching went on, just learning games. He brought his CD player to the school, and he showed them the motions to their favorite songs. Emily had put the mix together and recorded the songs. How he missed her. The classroom was not the same. He hated the way the second-grade teachers and Liz ganged up on her. He used to think they were nice women, but he was wrong.

When Emily was called down to Mrs. Voughn's office, red and pink blotches covered her face when she came out. He only saw her cry a handful of times growing up, and every time was because of her mother. Like the day her mother died and he held her so close, not ever wanting to let her go. Or the day her mother showed up at the beach sloppy drunk and told her to get in the car. Luckily his mom stepped in and drove her mother home. She insisted that Emily stay at the beach with them because she and Dawson were having such a good time. That time she cried in the ocean, and he held her close because her mother went through her room and sold her clothes without asking. Her mother ruined her life and made her feel guilty even though her mother's bad decisions drove her to her own death. He had wanted to take away her pain then and he still did.

During his prep time he head for the principal's office. It was time they had a little talk. Mrs. Voughn was only a couple years older than Emily and him, but she had a chip on her shoulder. She wanted to be a part of the second-grade clique, but because she was their boss she had to stay aloof. She was always protecting them and giving them what they wanted, but he never knew she was so callous. They all got together and went for walks, but she was careful not to get too close.

HE APPROACHED her in her office. She knew why he was there. She talked first because she knew he was not happy.

"Emily is replaceable. Her husband was a drug addict and Emily had to know. I don't want that kind of a role model in my school and around my students so don't you dare come in here to try to tell me any different. We all know PSA's are easily replaced."

"I've known Emily since we were children. She's a good person. This all started because Mrs. Eli was jealous of my relationship with Emily. It's none of her business what I do outside of work. You made a huge mistake firing her. She is not easily replaceable and neither are the other PSA's. I had no idea this was the person you were. I thought you were better than that."

She sneered at him. "Tell me, Dawson, are you a swinger?"

A swinger! He laughed. "No I'm not, nor is Emily. She's divorced now, but she was very upset when she found out about her husband's use."

Mrs. Voughn's eyes gleamed. "That doesn't mean you're not a swinger."

"I can't be a swinger because my wife is dead!" He did not want to lose his temper but she pushed him too far.

That stopped her in tracks. She swallowed her tongue and listened to him.

"PSA's are important for the kids and the teachers. Their connection with the children is critical to the children's development. Emily keeps us going. Without her help, I probably would not have survived the school year."

He crossed his arms and glared at her. "Now I want you to promise you're going to hire Emily back for next year, and to accept my relationship with Emily, whatever it becomes, is not against any rules and it really isn't any of your business."

"That is no way to talk to your superior."

She huffed and he held up his hand. "We won't flaunt it in the school if anything ever develops.

"But it's inappropriate."

"Why? There are married teachers in the school and in the middle school. Some of them even teach the same grades."

Still she hesitated.."Mrs. Eli has asked me out multiple times. If you're threatening Emily then you need to do the same to Mrs. Eli." He made a point of calling Liz Mrs. Eli in front of Mrs. Voughn to show her he was no different than a PSA, he just had a different job. Why she would not allow her to call Liz by her first name was ridiculous and prejudice when teachers were okay to call each other by their first names. He hated that she called Emily Mrs. Fredrickson because everyone knew PSA's went by Miss, followed by their first name.

That shut her up. Liz was also newly divorced, and she asked him out before her divorce was official.

He did not judge, but he had no idea the kind of person Liz was until Emily came around. Insecure and jealous were only a few of her traits. He had told her long ago that he was uninterested, but instead wanted to be friends. She had said she understood, but she was just another jealous woman wanting what she couldn't have.

All the teachers were going out to Side Lake to meet at Bimbo's Octagon for pizza and wings. The place was known for having the best pizza and wings around. "I need to get all the classroom decorations done first," he told the teachers after school as they planned the night out.

By the time he got home at seven, he was too exhausted to go anywhere. He fell asleep on the couch waiting to hear Emily's car pull into her driveway.

He woke up to loud voices and knocking on his door. He opened the door to the second-grade posse coming in to party. He wanted to tell them to leave, but he felt bad for ditching them earlier. They were his colleges and they brought beer and music.

Liz was the last one inside, holding a bottle of tequila. "Tequila straight from Mexico, worm and all," she said, holding the bottle above her head.

She howled and he shook his head and laughed.

Jan set a CD player on the kitchen counter and the beers in the fridge.

"You do realize it isn't the nineties anymore, right?"

Jan squeezed his cheek. "You are so cute, but no, see I push this button and my phone goes on this charger and it plays my music. It's Bluetooth, too, but this way looks better." She cranked up the music. "But I'm pretty sure you brought a CD player to school today."

He took another swig of his beer. "You guys can stay for a little while, okay? But some of us have an early bedtime."

Jan tipped his beer can, and it splashed all over him.

He looked over to Emily's house, but her cabin was still dark. Where had she gone? Was she back with Matthew? He wanted her to be happy. But since she came back into his life, he felt happy again. Losing his wife and his daughter was the hardest thing he had ever been through. Second worst thing was losing Emily.

He watched the teachers dance but all he could think about was Emily. The night they made love in Jordan's apartment was magical. They might have been drunk but he remembered every detail as if it were yesterday. He had moved on because she was Jordan's girlfriend. He waffled about how to tell Emily they could not be together when he wanted to tell her he loved her so he avoided the whole conversation.

He met Bobby at that fateful party. It was supposed to be a one-night thing. Who knew the slutty party girl was actually a pharmacy student letting loose for the first time since college? A girl who had too many beers and who lost her virginity to him in the bathroom.

Not the most romantic sex they ever had, but it led to five wonderful years with her. She would have a place in his heart forever. After she died, he never imagined being with anyone else until Emily came back into his life. She knew everything about him. She knew about his fear of alligators after they were chased by one in the neighbor's yard when they were ten. Emily had screamed, "Zig-zag!" but he was too panicked to react. Somehow he reached the door to his house and hid inside for three days. Emily had to bribe him to come outside. She checked all around the house for gators just like his mom did for monsters in his closet and under his bed when he was a child.

Emily never made fun of him for it. She knew his fear was serious and brought on post-traumatic stress disorder. If anyone found out about his phobia at school he would have been made fun of until the day he died. She hated snakes and spiders, and he hated gators. He killed spiders when she screamed that she saw one.

He secretly loved to watch *Ghost* with Emily, even though he told her he hated it. The love story fascinated him, and he liked the way Emily smiled when Patrick Swayze put his arms around Demi Moore as they sculpted a vase on her pottery wheel.

When he turned sixteen, he threw the DVD away because his dad found it and straight out asked him if he was gay. He said no, but his dad continued to make remarks about how it was okay if he was, that they would not judge him. When he married Bobby, his parents finally let go of their suspicions.

He wanted nothing more than to be a father, but he lost the chance of that when his wife and baby died right in front of him. He could do nothing to save them. He had cried as the doctors escorted him from the room so they could "do their job and try to save his family's lives."

The day they died he lost his faith in God. Everything happens for a reason, some people said. Why would God do this for a reason? What good would that do? His baby never even got to breathe in this world. What did his child do to deserve dying after only a few moments? That was not a God to him. Later, after he began teaching kindergarten, he slowly realized sometimes things just happen and maybe it was not the fault of God.

He had a passion for children, and teaching was the only thing that took his pain away. So many teachers told him he was crazy for teaching kindergarten, and he would hate it, but the children were the reason he woke up every morning.

They made his life worth living. In a way, they were his family.

He worried about them when they came to school in the same clothes, or when child protection showed up asking if he had any concern or worries about a child. Children were honest and loved to share with the class the crazy things that went on at home. One time a student announced to the class his father was in prison. Another child told the class that he sleeps under his bed because his mommy and daddy fight every night. Kindergartners were very honest and did not hold back. Next year he should keep a notebook close and write down the funny things they said every day. Their parents would be livid, but maybe they would start realizing their child heard and saw everything. If need be, he spoke to the parents if their child was having trouble at school or at home. It broke his heart when some parents did not care at all about their child's progress, but what hurt even more was custody battles. He watched the children used as pawns, and he just wanted to scoop them up and take them home.

Liz and Ellen pulled him into the middle of the living room to dance. Liz was twerking up and down the front of his body. He shook his head. This was not his opinion of fun, especially with how immature they were acting. Ellen sandwiched him from behind. He stood there drinking his beer. Then Liz squeezed his junk, and he backed away.

"Hey! You can dance without me."

"Oh, come on, it was just a little fun. Relax," Liz said.

Jan sauntered over and put her hands all over his neck. She held on and dipped herself. She held a glass of merlot in one hand. What kind of damage would it do if she got it on his white carpet? Bobby had chosen white carpeting even though he told her it was a bad idea, especially since they had a child on the way. She argued that white was the easiest to clean with bleach.

Liz pointed at the window and before he could look, Jan dumped her red wine all over the front of his white shirt. He jumped back.

"Oh, I'm such a klutz." Jan laughed. "Liz, would you mind helping Mr. K here take off his shirt while I get a paper towel to clean up my mess?"

Before he could object, he was blinded by the inside of his t-shirt. He was trying to hold up his beer and help her pull it off with his left hand. She finally got it off and threw it to Addie, who threw it into the kitchen sink. Jan ran over with a long line of paper towels and gave one to Liz and said, "This is for his body."

"Oh, you are bad," Liz said. She was half dabbing his chest with it, half squeezing him. He was not interested, but his body was not listening to his head. He grabbed the paper towel from her and did it himself so she would not notice.

This had to end. He needed a shower, and they were making him uncomfortable. "Okay, everybody, the party's over.

Liz wrapped her arms around him and looked out the window again, a smirk on her face. This time he followed her gaze. There at her cabin window stood a horrified Emily. How long had she been watching this act? These girls really knew how to put on a show. Colleagues or not, he was done with it. "Get out!" He had to shout to be heard over the music. "Get out, all of you."

Liz only squeezed his neck harder and pressed her wet lips against his and pushed her slimy tongue in his mouth. He pulled away and looked out the window in time to see Emily running outside. She got into her car and drove away.

He marched over to the DVD player and turned it off.

"Either you ladies get out now, or you are going to see a side of me you don't want to see."

And that was what it took for them to finally leave. But the damage was already done.

Liz licked her lips and gave him goo-goo eyes. "I'll come over tomorrow morning and help you clean this up."

"Don't you dare step foot into my house. You have done enough." He slammed the door in their faces.

CHAPTER 19

Emily

*C*ars were parked in Dawson's driveway. Who would be coming over at this time of night? He never had a lot of visitors. He liked his peace and quiet. Lights were on in his house. Liz, Jan, and the rest of the teacher clique were dancing in front of the bay window. Dawson was standing there while they were grinding all over him. Jan spilled her drink and Liz took off Dawson's shirt. Her hands were all over him.

"Buck up, girl. He's not yours to claim," she murmured.

The teacher clique was putting on an act for her benefit. When Mrs. Eli kissed Dawson, she started hyperventilating and had to get out fast.

Her breathing was back to normal by the time she reached Matthew's house, but her heart was still racing. She used her key to get in the door.

"Is Irene sleeping?"

"No, I went out to dinner so she stayed at Jillian's."

His eyes were glossy and red, and he avoided looking her in the eye.

She took a step back, her chest tight. "You haven't changed at all, have you? You're on drugs right now? Aren't you, Matthew?"

He shipped off their daughter so he could get high. What drug did he take? For the first time in her life, she wished she had experienced drugs so she could have more knowledge of the symptoms and the addiction. Why could he not just stay sober?

"I just smoked a little weed, that's all."

"I can't even talk to you right now, you disgust me. How are you going to be a dad when you're stuck in prison? What is probation going to say? Do you even care?"

She did not know him at all anymore. All they did was fight. Were they ever happy? Was he always this selfish?

He grabbed her arm.

"Don't touch me! You need help, you know that?"

He chased her out the door. "Don't go, please don't go."

She was already gone.

She called Gabby and Jillian and cried into the phone about how stupid she was for thinking it could work. All he cared about was himself.

"I saw him tonight with a girl," Gabby said. "I guess she worked at the prison when he was there. He said he was just friends with her but our argument got heated and he took off and left the woman at the restaurant."

He'd already moved on? He just told her he was trying to make things work. "I'm so stupid."

Gabby sighed.

"I hate to admit this, but you and Jillian were right. Our relationship is toxic."

Gabby could have said, I told you so and rubbed it in her face, but she was quiet.

"I should have listened to you guys. It's over, isn't it?"

"I don't know, Em. He has a problem much bigger than you should take on."

She did not need a man in her life. Screw Matthew and screw Dawson too. She would have to deal with Matthew for the rest of her life because of Irene, but he would no longer be her responsibility.

She called the probation office and left a message. She did not know who he was on probation with, but they would get the message. He needed to learn there were consequences for his actions. Gabby and Jillian agreed.

She waited for her lungs to get heavy after Gabby told her he was out on a date. She thought the tears would fall, but she felt nothing. She felt nothing for him at all. She loved him as Irene's dad, but not as her lover or her husband, not anymore.

"Em, stay at Jillian's with me and the kids," Gabby said when she called her back.

"No, I want to go home and sleep in my bed." But where exactly was her home? At Matthew's family cabin? She did not care, she just wanted the quiet, the darkness of the dock at night on Side Lake. She wanted to look up at the stars in the sky and breathe in the fresh night air. The breeze would keep the mosquitoes away. As for Dawson, he was a grown man, and if he wanted to be with Liz or Jan, she was done caring. He had broken her heart too many times.

DAWSON'S CAR was gone when she got home. Too bad she did not have a garage to put her car in so he would not know she was home. She needed a bottle of wine and her feet in the water. After months of living on a lake, she would never be able to live in town again.

Growing up, Ft. Myers was beautiful, but she was at peace here in Northern Minnesota. The ocean left salt on beach homes, and she would never miss the hurricanes and tornadoes she endured growing up in Florida. Hibbing rarely had tornadoes due to the mines surrounding it. They protected the Iron Range. Some people called the Range a giant hole in the Earth.

Small towns sucked because everyone knew everyone's business, but she needed to stop caring what they thought. The town meant well and neighbors kept an eye on each other's homes, and they took care of one another through grief and loss. If someone bought a car, the neighbors did not one up them like they did in Florida. Maybe this place was not so bad. Side Lake was her home now, even if she couldn't live in this cabin forever. She spent so many years comparing Florida and Minnesota.

She set down her bottle of wine on the dock and stopped just as she was about to pour it into her glass. Would drinking really solve her problems, or was she just numbing the pain like Matthew? She pushed the alcohol aside. No drinking unless it was a celebration. Maybe she understood Matthew's addiction with numbing the pain just a little.

He was Jillian's responsibility now. This was supposed to be Matthew's time with Irene, but until he was negative of all substances, Irene would be staying away from him.

She took off her sandals and dipped her feet in the water. It was chilly but refreshing. She pulled her feet out and lay down on the dock. She could not do this anymore. She no longer wanted to be with Matthew, nor did he want to be with her.

Happiness was not something she needed to search for in

a man, a job, or where she lived. Happiness was a mindset that she had to take control of. "As of this moment, I am going to be happy." She closed her eyes and found her solace in nature right there before her.

CHAPTER 20

*E*mily dug out her black, one-piece swimsuit and grabbed a towel. Her hot pink bikini with white polka-dots lay crumpled in the bottom of the drawer. She smiled. The suit was one of the first purchases she made when she moved to Minnesota. Back then she had a flat stomach and when she flexed, her abs showed four pockets of solid muscle. Beach volleyball and a high metabolism had a lot to do with the way she looked. She could eat what she wanted and never gained a pound. Then she got pregnant, but she still wore the bikini when she moved to San Francisco to live with her sister, Jamie. She was so comfortable in her own skin back then.

It hurt to think about that year, the worst year of her life. She shut off the memories as best she could, and she made Jamie and her husband promise to keep her secret. Jamie swore she would never tell, and as far as she knew, Jamie was true to her word. She had wanted to tell Matthew. She tried so many times, but she always panicked. She hated the distance she kept from her family, and she hated not returning to San Francisco because she wanted to forget it ever happened. She wanted to forget what she did.

She put the one piece down and picked up her bikini. It had been years since she wore it, but she was going to wear it again tonight. She was going to regain the confidence she had so long ago.

She held in her stomach as she turned from side to side in her full-length mirror. Sure she was slim, but she was still jiggly. Stretch marks and a flat butt. But she was who she was because she was a mom and proud of it.

She stepped outside in just her suit, and the chilly air sent goosebumps all over her arms and legs. She wrapped the towel around her body and walked to the dock. She sat down on the edge, her feet dangling in the water. How deep was the water here? Was it as shallow as McCarthy's? Only one way to find out. She jumped off the dock feet first. Memories of the first time she jumped off Dawson's diving board and blacked out flashed through her mind on the way down. This time no one was around to save her if she panicked. The water hit her like a block of ice, and her feet hit the sand. The water was just above her imperfect belly button.

"Breathe Emily, breathe," she said. Her lungs refused to expand. They were already full from the shock of the cold on her body. She dove under the water and swam out a little farther. The dark was a bit creepy, but the water did not hide anything scary, like a shark or a jellyfish, and the stars lit up the sky. She closed her eyes and dove under again, still chilly, but her body was adjusting and her lungs were expanding.

The water lit up around her. She jumped and turned around. Dawson's outside light had turned on. She put up her hand against the blinding light.

"Emily, Emily is that you?"

Her eyes followed a dark shadow making its way down to

his dock. She could hear each step beneath his feet as the wood creaked.

"Yes," she said.

"Can I talk to you ... about earlier? I didn't realize you were watching, it wasn't what it looked like."

"You really don't need to say anything, I saw enough."

He ran back to land and up her dock. The dock shook and made terrible noises as if it was going to topple into the water. He stood over her. "It wasn't what it looked like, I swear. They just showed up and--"

"I really don't want to hear it. It doesn't matter anyways we aren't even together. In case you're wondering, Matthew is back and I'm happy." A little lie.

"I respect that and I'm happy for you. I would never want to break up your family. I just want you to be happy. This doesn't change things with Jan, Liz, and those teachers. They're my friends and nothing more."

"Like I said, I don't care."

She dipped under the water again. Maybe he would be gone when she came up. She held her breath and got out as far as she could with one underwater breaststroke. When she came up he was still there, only farther away. She went under again, not coming up until her lungs felt like they were going to explode. She couldn't touch the bottom and she was so far out, she could only see his outline on the dock. The water was black and her heart began to beat out of control. She tensed up and panicked.

A cramp hit her leg and she sank below the surface. She gasped for air each time she surfaced, but she was swallowing too much water. She needed to take control of her breathing, but the water was choking her, and she kept sinking deeper. She cried out in pain at the cramp, and her arms flailed and splashed against the water. If she drowned, Matthew would have to raise Irene. No way was she going to let that happen. She fought to keep her head up, and tried to float on her back. But every time she straightened her leg the pain sank her.

Something pulled at her waist. Dawson's arm was wrapped tightly under her arm pits and over her chest. He was squeezing her so hard her ribs might crack. He was on his back and breathing heavily as he kicked them to shore. She was coughing and spitting up water, her nose and throat burning.

He lifted her onto the dock. She rolled on her side and coughed up more water. Her mind flashed back to his swimming pool when she had blacked out, and she remembered someone pulling her to the side of the pool, and squeezing her ribs so tight they were sore for days. She never talked about who pulled her out of the pool because she was embarrassed. But it was Dawson who saved her in the pool, it was Dawson who saved her on the side of the road after her accident, and it was Dawson who saved her from drowning tonight. Why was it always him? Would she be dead without him? Probably. The thought made her laugh out loud, even though her throat was sore and her breathing was so heavy it burned her lungs.

He lay down next to her on the dock, his legs dangling in the water. He was weak like her, exhausted and breathing hard. He started laughing, Their laughter got louder until they both turned their heads and stared at each other in the moonlight.

He ran his fingers through her long, snarled hair. "Are you okay?" he whispered.

"You saved me that day in the pool, didn't you?"

He did not have to answer, she already knew.

"I went to see Matthew after I saw the strip show."

He sat up, his arm resting on his leg. "I'm never going to live that down, am I?

"I lied about being happy with him. He was high, Dawson. I really wanted our family to work, but I can't push what isn't there."

"I'm sorry," he said.

"You don't need to be sorry. I'm sorry I lied."

They lay in silence and gazed up at the stars, still too exhausted to move.

"Why is it that we keep running into each other and you keep saving my life? It's almost as if fate keeps pushing us toward each other for some reason."

She sat up, still a little dizzy. He put his arm around her to support her, but pulled away when she sat up. "It does seem that way, doesn't it?"

She gave him a gentle punch in the shoulder and stood up. Had she ever stopped loving him? But if he found out what she did in San Francisco, he would never forgive her. He would run away and never look back. So she tried not to get close, but they always found their way back to each other.

"I need to go to bed, I'm exhausted." She wobbled in the direction of her cabin, still a bit unsteady.

He followed close behind, his arm under the small of her back. "I'll walk you up. Are you sure you don't need to see a doctor?"

"I'm fine, but I do think I need an escort."

He turned on the lights and followed her into her room. She was limping from the reoccurring charlie horse in her calf. "Ouch, my calf keeps cramping up. I can't stand on it. I need to lay down."

"You need to get out of that wet suit, it can't be comfortable."

She lay down on the bed, still holding her leg. He tried to rub the cramp out, but she cried in pain. He pulled her toes back and she winced, but took short breaths to calm down.

He rubbed her gently, trying to straighten her leg, but it cramped again.

"Where are your pajamas?"

"In the second drawer with my t-shirts and underwear."

Here she was sprawled out on her back with all her body image issues in full sight and she felt no need to cover up. She trusted him and she saw absolutely no judgment on his face, only concern.

He grabbed a scarf off her hook next to the closet and brought it, along with her long t-shirt and panties to the bed. "I'll tie this scarf around my eyes so I can help you."

"But then you won't be able to see what you're doing."

He dropped the scarf on the floor. His inner struggle was obvious as he shut his eyes and took a deep breath. "I will do my best to be professional."

He gently rolled her on her side and unfastened the clasp, then rolled her back. He pulled the straps down her arms, and she held the bikini top to her chest as he slipped the shirt over her head and over her upper body. When she was fully covered, she pulled one arm through while holding her leg steady with the other, then switched.

She bridged her back as he turned his head and pulled down her wet bottoms. One leg and then the next. She held back a giggle. He looked so uncomfortable with his eyes squeezed tight. He tossed the bottoms on the floor, and she slid her legs though her underwear. Then he pulled them up as she bridged her hips. He took the suit to the bathroom, then headed down the hall to get her meds for the pain in her leg.

He shook out a couple Aleve and handed her a glass of water. "How's the leg?"

"Still hard to straighten, but it's okay right now. I think I just need some sleep."

He covered her legs with the blanket and kissed her on

173

the forehead. She put her arms around his neck, and pulled him closer. He pulled back, and she moved her hands underneath his shirt. He stood up.

"I want this so bad, but I don't want you to regret it."

She looked into his eyes. Desire for her shone in them. A moan escaped his lips and he walked to the door. "Your phone is next to the bed, call me if you need anything."

She nodded and smiled at him. "Always such a gentleman. Thank you, Dawson."

He turned the light off. "I think I'm going to take a cold shower now."

She laughed, but she could tell that was exactly what he needed.

JUNE

CHAPTER 21

Dawson

*D*awson heard her car pull out of the driveway early the next morning. About an hour later, he was getting out of the shower, standing in the kitchen with no shirt, and wiping his hair dry when a car drove up. Could she be back already? An unfamiliar car pulled into the driveway and a man stepped out. He was handsome and muscular build. Not as tall as him, but the man definitely hit the weight room, but it also looked like he skipped leg day.

This must be Matthew.

The stranger lifted up the rug, probably looking for a hidden key, and then searched under the nearby rocks.

Dawson stepped outside. "Excuse me, are you looking for Emily?"

The man turned around and stared at him. "You must be Dawson."

Emily told Matthew about him? He moved closer and stuck out his hand. "And you must be Matthew."

"Where is Emily?"

It was more of a demand than a question.

" I saw her take off a while ago, I'm sure she'll be back soon. Want to come in for some coffee?"

Matthew followed him inside the house. He whistled. "You know, this used to be a little hole in the wall cabin. It had one room and no running water when I was a kid. When I was a teenager, they started building this mansion. It's really something, isn't it?"

He glanced at his home from a different perspective, trying to see if through Matthew's eyes. He was in it every day so he took its beauty for granted. After he lost Bobby, he hated the place for a while and wanted to sell it. He still wanted to sell it so he could move on with his life. "They did a good job. Please, have a seat."

Matthew sat down at the breakfast bar that connected to the counter running along the enormous kitchen wall.

He commented on the layout and knew a lot more than the average man. Dawson was impressed.

"Are you a carpenter?" Dawson said. "Your knowledge of structure is impressive."

"Nah, but I always wanted to be. Anyway, Emily tells me the two of you have been spending a lot of time together. You are neighbors and grew up together, right?"

"Well, we also worked together."

Beads of sweat collected on Matthew's forehead. He was getting worked up about something.

"I don't know what you think is going on here, but you're just her rebound. She's my wife, and I think it's in your best interest to back off before you get hurt."

"I thought you were divorced now?" Dawson said. He watched as Matthew's hands turned to fists.

"She told me about your kiss."

Dawson almost fell off his chair. "She did?"

"She's confused right now. You know she tells me everything."

No way was he going to play Matthew's game. There were so many things he wanted to say to this man but he bit his tongue.

"You aren't a man of many words, are you?"

Matthew moved closer, his eyes burning a hole through Dawson's head. This was turning into trouble.

Dawson put his hand up. "I want no trouble, man. I have nothing but respect for you. It sounds like you and Emily are going through some stuff, so maybe she's the one you need to talk to."

Emily stood in the doorway. "Dawson, is Matthew here?"

Matthew dropped his fists and put on a happy face for Emily. "This conversation isn't over," he muttered.

Emily locked eyes with Dawson. "Is everything okay here?"

"It's fine, we were just having a little chat." Matthew practically pushed her out the door. "Let's talk at the cabin. "Bye, Dawson. It was great meeting you," he said with absolute sarcasm.

Dawson watched as they walked to her cabin and went inside. Was she taking him back?

CHAPTER 22

*E*mily turned to Matthew once they were in the cabin. "Okay, what did you say?"

"Nothing. I don't understand what you see in that guy."

"What are you talking about? This is more about you than it is me, and you know it. I called your probation officer and told him you were high."

He scowled. "I know."

"You aren't going to yell at me for getting you into trouble, which could send you back in prison?"

"Emily, I smoked some pot, it wasn't like meth or something. It's really not a big deal."

The heat rose in her cheeks.

He grabbed onto her hand. She pulled away.

"I'm not saying pot is okay. I wasn't thinking. I saw Gabby and she pissed me off so I ran off to get high and like I said, it could have been meth but I turned it down.

"So every time someone gets you angry, you're going to use again? Grow up!"

"No, that's not what I'm saying. I screwed up. It won't happen again."

"And what did your sister do that made you so angry?"

"I was out eating dinner with a woman, and she assumed I was on a date."

Emily was silent for an uncomfortable length of time.

"I wasn't on a date. She's my sponsor, but Gabby never bothered to ask. She took me outside and starting throwing my past in my face. I'm used to lifting weights to calm me, but that wasn't an option so I did the only other thing I was used to. I went searching for drugs."

Why did he think this was okay?

Her leg collapsed and she groaned in pain. She grabbed her leg and hopped to the table.

He dropped to the floor beside her. "What happened?"

"I got a leg cramp swimming last night. It's been fine all morning but now it's acting up again."

He sat down next to her at the table as she rubbed it. "When did you go swimming last night? By yourself or with that piece of crap next door?"

How like him to overreact after he went on a date with a woman. Sponsor or not, he did not mention it to her, which meant he was hiding it from her. "Are you really jealous or are you trying to take the spotlight off you for going on a date?"

"Does it bother you to think I was on a date?"

"Honestly? No. I worry about you using with the stress of a new relationship, but I'm not jealous of someone else."

For the first time she realized their relationship would never be the same again.

"So that's it? We're over?" he said. "It's because of that Dawson guy isn't it?"

"Dawson and I have a past, but you and I have been trying to rekindle something that's long gone. I'm not seeing Dawson."

"And I'm not seeing Becky."

She smiled. "So she has a name."

"Of course she has a name."

It was okay for him to have a relationship with this woman, but it wasn't okay that she talked to Dawson. Typical.

"I don't want Irene hanging around that guy, okay?"

Did he think he could tell her who she could and could not see? "I don't think it's your call. I wouldn't bring anyone around Irene if I wasn't sure they were good people. I've known Dawson forever. He's a kindergarten teacher, for goodness sake."

Matthew laughed at her. "It makes sense now that I think about it."

"And he owns his own construction company."

That shut Matthew up because she knew that was his dream job.

"If we aren't getting back together we need to start co-parenting, Matthew, I mean it. No more jealousy. If you like this Becky lady you need to make sure it's serious before Irene finds out she's your girlfriend."

He stared at his hands before he finally said, "I'm going to take my recovery seriously, and I'm not going to have a girl-friend for a year. Becky was a corrections officer at the prison, and she's my friend and my sponsor. I need to focus on me right now."

SHE WAS BLOWN AWAY. Was he really starting to change? Maybe he was finally starting to grow up and take responsibility for his actions. She wanted to believe last night was just a stumble on his way down the long road of recovery. "You have no idea how glad I am to hear you say that." Emily hugged him. "If you need anything, I am always going to be here for you."

"Do you think it would be swallowing my pride if I asked Dawson to hire me as a carpenter?"

She pushed him. "Yes, but do it. You're on your own with this one, buddy."

"But didn't you just say if I needed anything, you would always be there for me?"

"Ha! Good try," she said. "Now get out of here."

He closed the gap between them and gave her a hug and a kiss on the cheek. "Don't ever think I didn't love you because I did. I love you Emily."

The end of their relationship was so sad, but she had no regrets. They were going to be okay.

CHAPTER 23

*A*fter Matthew left, Dawson came in without knocking. "Everything okay?"

Emily raised an eyebrow. "I'm sorry about Matthew."

"Ah, I get it. I don't blame him. I'd be pissed too if I thought some guy was moving in on my woman."

"I'm not his woman," she said. "But if you must know, I think he's going to be sucking up to you after today."

"Why's that?"

"Well, I think he was hoping you'd give him a job. It's been his life-long dream to be a carpenter." That sounded too pushy. Dawson should not feel obligated to give Matthew a job. "But I mean you don't have to, it's no big deal."

"I may be able to arrange something."

"Seriously, Dawson, it's no big deal if you don't."

He just smiled.

Her phone rang and Dad showed up on the face. Dawson was looking over her shoulder and nodded his head as if telling her she should answer it. She shook her head, then on a whim she answered. "Hi, dad."

She walked into her bedroom and shut the door.

. . .

"You actually answered," he said.

Her heart sank. She was a terrible daughter always avoiding him but she wanted to forget that part of her life.

"I'm coming to visit you and my granddaughter."

He was not asking, he was telling. "Okay," was all she could muster.

"My plane will be in Duluth at ten in the morning. Lindsey is coming with me."

"Lindsey? You know dad, the normal way to do this is to ask and plan," she said.

"Well, if you would answer your damn phone maybe I would. I'm not taking no for an answer. I'm coming to see you. Don't worry, we're renting a car so you don't need to pick me up. We won't be a hassle at all."

"You're my family, you won't be a hassle," she said.

She walked out of the bedroom to find Dawson lingering near the door. "Everything okay?"

He could always read her. "No, my dad is flying in tomorrow and he just now told me. I need to get this cabin cleaned up.

"Well, I have to go to work, but afterward I'm coming back to help you."

She tried to object but he added, "I'm not taking no for an answer."

What was with people today? "Okay, I could use the help. Thanks."

"Did you tell him I'm your neighbor?"

She shook her head. "I guess he will find out soon enough."

Her father was also going to find out she was newly divorced and unemployed. This would be tough. She was not ready to see them, but like the man said, he was not taking no for an answer.

DAWSON CAME BACK AROUND eight o'clock, but she was pretty much done cleaning.

"This place looks amazing," he said. "I'm sorry I'm so late."

She finished wiping off the counter. "It really wasn't that bad."

"Let me wash up, and I'll take you out in my boat and we'll watch the sunset."

That was exactly what she needed. Her hands had been shaking and her insides in turmoil as she worried about her family coming to visit. Realistically, she could only hide for so long before they found her. It would all be okay as long as her secret remains hidden.

THE LAKE WAS STILL, and the loons were yodeling in the water as Dawson started the engine. She sat on the seat next to him, taking in the wind and the shimmering water. The rocky shorelines bordered the birch, pine, and aspen forest. The sun was slipping below the horizon. The atmospheric refraction distorted the sun's rays and colors of orange, pink, and yellow scattered throughout the sky, illuminating a trembling path across the lake water.

Dawson stopped the boat in the middle of Big Sturgeon and handed Emily a can of seltzer water. She cracked it open. The sound echoed in the silent night.

"This is so beautiful," she said, taking a big gulp of her water. "Thank you for taking me out."

"I don't want you to get the wrong idea, this isn't a date," he said with a playful smile.

"Oh you wish," she said. "What makes you think I'm

interested?"

"Ouch. You really know how to kill a guy's ego. So are you and Matthew done done?"

"Yes, but he's Irene's father so he will always be around," she said.

She was glad for the closure between her and Matthew before she started anything new. She was not sure she was ready to dive into something with Dawson just yet. How long would he wait for her?

THEY ROAD back to shore and he tied up the boat.

"Thank you for the amazing night, you helped me forget about everything and just relax. You have always been that person, thank you."

He grabbed her hand. "Come with me, there's something I want to show you."

He led her into his house and opened the last door on the right. The yellow and green room had a duck and frog border around it. This was going to be their baby's nursery. The thought made her heart sink.

He removed a white sheet from some sort of object. "Over here."

Her excitement sucked the air right out of her lungs. "Oh my gosh, you didn't? I can't believe it." It was a pottery wheel just like the one from *Ghost*. She beamed.

He pulled out a bench and placed it in front of the pottery wheel. "Sit."

"SADDLE THE BENCH," he said as she sat down.

Excitement squealed out of her throat. "Okay, Okay,what do I do now?" she said. "I've never actually done this before, Dawson."

He was staring at his phone.

She laughed. "Don't tell me you have to google it."

"Just be patient," he said. "You're ruining the moment."

She made a zipper signal over her mouth. Her legs and arms shook with excitement. *Unchained Melody* played on his phone. He plugged it into the speaker on the end table and she inched over so he had room to sit right behind her.

"I can't believe it, you're even playing the Righteous Brothers. You know this is my dream." She could not calm down or contain her excitement. This was really happening. "My favorite movie is actually coming to life.

"Our favorite movie," he said

She got up and turned around, taking off his shirt. "If we're going to do this, you need to be perfect."

"You don't think I'm perfect already?"

She shot him an annoyed look. "Stop."

He placed the clay on the bat with the tip pointed down. He guided her hands to tap to the center while the wheel turned slowly.

"We're doing it," she said.

He just shook his head. "Focus."

He guided her hands into the bowl of water all set up for them and then began pushing the clay forward. He pushed his body against hers until the inside of her legs were touching the wheel.

"Now anchor your elbows tightly against your body."

"That sounds so dirty," she said.

She followed, her elbows tucked in tight to her abdomen. They began coning down the clay and then he took the lead with his right hand on top of the cone, interlocking with his left hand. He grabbed her hand again and led her right hand to push down and her left to push forward as he sped up the wheel.

Her heart beat rapidly, and her body tensed as she closed

her eyes and let him lead her. The clay felt slimy but soft beneath her hands. This was so much harder than it looked.

"Now put your thumbs in the center to mark it," he said.

She did what she was told. They made a hole in the center and wet their hands again.

"When did you learn how to do this?"

"I took a class in college. I always dreamed that someday I would get to teach you, just like this."

The clay collapsed and she turned around and saddled the bench, facing him. She wrapped her gooey hands around his neck and rubbed the clay under his eyes like a football player with eye-black on.

He put his finger on her nose and drew cat whiskers on her cheeks.

"Hey," she said in a banter voice.

He held still as she covered his face with the clay on her hands. The muck drying to her skin and hardening. She grabbed the clay off the wheel and put a lump of it on his head.

As he reached for it, she playfully restrained his hands and then he leaned in and kissed her. A dreamy kiss that stopped their play. They fell to the floor and rolled around, getting the clay all over the carpet, but he did not seem to care.

He stared into her eyes. "I love you, Emily."

She squirmed away and got to her feet. She wanted more than anything to make love to this man, but she was afraid. "See you tomorrow?"

His smile turned into a sad frown as he nodded back at her.

"Goodnight, Dawson."

"Goodnight."

CHAPTER 24

*H*er father would arrive any time now. He was staying for three days and Lindsey was coming with him. She paced the cabin. It was now one o'clock in the afternoon and still no word. She tried calling him again and this time he answered.

"Hello, sweet girl. I'm running a little late. Plans changed and I ended up flying into Minneapolis and renting a car because the plane to Duluth was delayed. It's about a five-hour drive?"

"Three and a half to Side Lake, Dad. I could have picked you guys up."

"That's okay, I can't wait to see you and your new place. Oh, and one other change of plans. Do you have room for two more?"

Who else could be coming with them? She never talked to anyone in Ft. Myers anymore. "Dad, who is with you?"

"Well, Jamie and Josie wanted to fly in from San Francisco and surprise you, but I told them you would need time to arrange for more people coming. So I just wanted to give you a heads up."

She dropped the phone and collapsed on the floor. She needed to get in her car and run away, never to look back. Josie and Jamie were coming? No, this was not happening. She ran into the kitchen and took out a brown lunch bag. She stuck her head in the bag and breathed into it before she passed out.

GABBY WAS SUPPOSED to go back to Duluth with Travis, but when Emily called her in tears and hyperventilating, she changed her plans.

Emily was on speakerphone and she could hear Gabby talking to Jillian.

"Go to her," Jillian said. "I'll take you to Duluth tomorrow. Travis can leave with the kids."

"Thank you, Jillian, you're a life saver. Olivia will watch the kids. I haven't asked her in a while."

GABBY STORMED into Emily's house without knocking. "What's going on?"

She was curled in a fetal position on the floor. She refused to call her father back. When he called she did not pick up the phone. What could she say other than turn around?

"I can't talk about it. It's that bad. Everyone is going to hate me, they're going to find out."

"Find out what?"

She wanted to tell her. Gabby would not judge or tell anyone. This was her sister's way of letting her know she was not going to keep her secret anymore. The voicemails said it all. "Emily, it's me again. I can't live with this secret anymore, the lies are killing me. I can't keep hiding this from our family, my daughter. It's time to come clean." It was all about

Jamie as usual. What about her? What was so wrong with honoring her promise?

"WILL you just sit here with me? Tell me when they come?" Emily said.

A car door slammed an hour later. Thank goodness Dawson was working a construction job. He wouldn't be back until late. He was off tomorrow and they had plans to go boating. He wanted to teach her to waterski. But now that was done.

She stood up, wiped her eyes, looked in the mirror, and smiled at Gabby. "Do I look okay?"

"I'm so confused, but yes you always do."

Emily straightened her shirt in the front and answered the door.

AS THE HOURS TICKED AWAY, Jamie never brought up the subject, and she slowly relaxed. Jamie would not just blurt it out to everyone. She needed to find a way to get her alone and convince her it was best to keep her secret a secret. After all, she did promise.

This was the first time she was seeing Josie since she was a baby. She was a beautiful girl and looked so much like her father. She was polite and kept asking when she would be able to meet Irene.

Emily avoided eye contact. "Matthew is bringing her home before bedtime."

Josie clapped her hands and her eyes sparkled. "I'm so excited to meet her."

She took her dad down to the dock and borrowed two of Dawson's fishing poles.

"So, my sweet girl, this is a beautiful place you have here."

Her father had not changed much over the years. She grabbed the minnow bucket and handed it to him. "Thanks, dad."

He stopped her and gazed deep into her eyes. "What's going on, Em? Why are you avoiding our calls?"

"I've just had a lot going on. Time goes by so fast."

He shook his head. "No, what's really going on? Do you blame me for your mother's death? You haven't been around for so long and when you did come visit you were so distant and you didn't even want to bring your husband along." He looked out to the lake.

She needed to be honest. "Dad, I blame you as much as I blame myself. You enabled her and looked the other way. I was so caught up in myself, I didn't even realize she was an addict. Why didn't you get her help?"

He handed her his fishing pole and paced up and down the dock until he finally stopped in front of her. "I ask myself those questions every day. Not so much now as I did back then. No one is responsible for what she did. She didn't want help. Don't you think I tried?"

She scowled. "Not hard enough."

"I loved your mom but none of us could save her. She had her own demons and I've made peace with that, you need to, too."

He sat back down and placed his hand on top of hers. "Forgive yourself and quit punishing your family." He hesitated. "But there's something else you're hiding, isn't there?"

Looking into his eyes, she saw the familiarity of her own eyes. She had been punishing him all these years, but it wasn't his fault. "I'm sorry, daddy," she said. "I know it isn't your fault but I just wish—"

"Wishing won't get you anywhere. Let it go. She loved you, you know that. I love you so let me in, please."

She missed these talks with her dad. She missed watching

movies and seeing who could be the first person to catch mistakes made in them. She missed how he'd laugh too loud in movie theaters, and how they always went out for strawberry cones after the movie. She wanted him to be a part of her life, of Irene's life.

"I was so stupid, I'm sorry," she said.

He put his arm around her. "I'm your dad, I forgive you no matter what. Life throws a lot at us but it's how you react that matters."

She had tears in her eyes and so did he. She nuzzled her head into his shoulder.

"So, where is your husband tonight?" He looked around as if Matthew was hiding somewhere close by.

"Well, we kind of split up. It's a long story."

He took the news calmly. "I'm sure if you split up it was for a good reason. Is he a good dad to Irene?"

"Yes, he is. He has some obstacles to overcome, but he's working hard."

He put a minnow on her line and cast it out for her like he did when she was five years old. She dipped her toes into the water once she had the rod back in her hand, just like when she was a child.

He stopped looking in the water for fish and looked deep into her eyes again.

"He was an addict like mama. I tried to fix him."

"Sounds like you're still a smart girl for getting out of it," he said. "I'm so sorry I wasn't there for you when your mother died."

He pulled their lines out. "Okay that's enough fishing."

"Let's go over to Dawson's dock. It's nicer."

They sat on the bench together. She pushed the dock with her feet so the articulating bench swung above the water, and their legs dangled over the small waves. Her dad looked impressed.

"Daddy, why did you buy drugs for mom when she was alive?"

The question caught him off guard. He took off his baseball cap and scratched his head. "How did you know about that?"

She laughed. "Dad, you took me with you. I had to wait in the car, and I was so scared."

Her father's face crumpled. "I'm so sorry, sweetheart. I never meant to scare you. I was stupid, and tired of fighting her so I did what she asked. I'm truly sorry you had to grow up that way. I didn't resent you running away after that. Hell, I would have done the same thing."

He kissed her on the forehead, and she snuggled into the crane of his neck like a child again.

"I did something really bad, too, daddy. I'm really scared it's going to ruin my life forever."

He turned his head to look at her, and she felt his breath on her face. He smelled of sunflower seeds and hot peppers. The scent took her back to her childhood and the way her mother yelled at him for spitting the sunflower seeds out in his truck.

"One thing I've learned in all my years on this earth is that you need to embrace your past and move on. You can't be at peace until you have nothing to hide. Mistakes are in the past, forgive yourself, sweet girl. If others can't forgive you then that's their problem. We aren't meant to keep secrets, they build up and we live in regret. You have always been a tough girl. When you made this so-called bad choice, did you do it with the intent to hurt others?"

She lifted her head. "No."

EMILY and her dad went back to the cabin.

"Let's take a walk and talk, Em," Jamie said.

"Please, can't I go with you for a walk?" Josie said.

Emily shook her head. "You need to be here to surprise Irene, remember?"

Josie smiled. "Okay. Auntie Emily, I'm so glad I finally got to meet you. My mom talks about you all the time."

Josie's words stayed with her as she led the way down Greenrock Road to Sixberry's Landing across the bridge. They sat in the dirt, and stared into the water. They had a perfect view of Dawson's house and both their docks.

"This place is so beautiful. When I learned you were living in Minnesota I thought of cold weather and being able to see for miles," Jamie said.

"It's definitely cold in the winter, but the summers get very hot and humid. Unbearable, really."

She knew it was coming in the way Jamie's body stiffened. The time to address the issue had arrived, and they both knew it would become a tense conversation.

"I know it was rude of me to just show up like this, unannounced, but you weren't answering my phone calls."

Because she wanted to avoid anything that had to do with her sister. It brought back too many bad feelings and Jamie knew this, or so she thought. "I know and I'm sorry. I wanted to put my past behind me and talking to you brought it all back when you kept asking for me to let you tell the truth. I'm sorry I put that on you. I thought I told you that."

"All I know is, I can't keep your secret any longer, I just can't."

Her heart was racing but she tried to stay calm. "You promised me you wouldn't tell anyone. You were the one who talked me into this. You can't go back on it now."

"It's not about you anymore, Emily. Josie needs to know the truth."

"Give me a day to think about it, okay? You remember my friend Dawson from when we were kids?"

"Yeah, the only friend you had as a child?"

"Yes, well it's a long story, but he lives in that big house next to mine." She pointed. "The one with the bench on the dock."

"Seriously? He lives right next door? Small world but don't change the subject."

"Just listen. He wanted me to go boating with him tomorrow, and he'd love to see you guys. Let's spend the day relaxing in the sun and water skiing. It's supposed to be a beautiful day, and then I'll tell her, okay? Or we can tell her together."

"Promise? Emily, if you don't tell her tomorrow then I will. I came all the way out here to give you the chance to do it in person."

"I know and I will. I promise."

CHAPTER 25

The day started off a little cloudy, but by nine in the morning the sun was shining over the lake.

Jamie joined her on the deck. "You get to stare at this view every morning, I'm so jealous."

"If only it was my cabin. I'm going to get an apartment in town after this summer now that Matthew and I are not getting back together."

"What happened with the two of you?"

If she had talked to Jamie a couple weeks ago, she would have told her Matthew was a jerk, a user, and selfish for not letting her help him. She did not understand the addiction her mom and Matthew struggled with, but she knew she could not fix them. "We grew apart, I guess you could say. It's for the best."

Jamie squeezed her shoulders. "I'm sorry. I can't wait to go boating and see Dawson after all these years."

Thankfully, Jamie changed the subject. She did not want to think about Dawson right now. After last night, she needed to clear her head and decide if she was ready for the next step with Dawson. She felt terrible for leaving him when it was getting so hot and heavy between them. Just thinking about it made her skin tingle.

"Are you feeling ready to tell Josie?"

"As ready as I'll ever be."

"It's going to be okay, I promise. It's hard for me, too. When she finds out I've been telling her lies all these years, I wonder if she will ever speak to me again."

"You're her mom," Emily said. "She doesn't have a choice."

She put Jamie to work making turkey and peanut butter and jelly sandwiches. She packed chips and treats and a cooler of water. She put Lindsey to work getting towels and sunscreen and watching Irene. Lindsey avoided looking her in the eye but followed her directions.

Gabby had driven back to Duluth early in the morning without learning the secret. She had hugged her and whispered, "I'll tell you when I'm ready." That was the thing about Gabby, she always respected her boundaries. Their friendship was easy, trusting, and never any jealousy. She learned the hard way jealousy only leads to a competition that no one wins. Mrs. Eli came to mind.

Emily packed up the boat with towels and counted the life jackets. Dawson was strapping an extra gas can to the back of the boat. She wore her one piece and brought a white t-shirt in case it got too hot. She had sun-kissed freckles to show for her lack of sunscreen when she was young. Who knew you should reapply every two hours instead of just once a day?

She turned around to get off the boat and almost ran into Dawson.

He wasn't moving. Just grinning. "Are you ready for a day full of boating?"

"More than ever. I've never water skied before, you know."

"Really? You'll be awesome." He looked her up and down.

"Where's the pink bikini?"

Her face grew hot at the memory of him taking it off her.

He took her hand as she climbed out of the boat. She stepped onto the dock and looked back. "What pink bikini?"

Her dad, Jamie, and Josie sat in the back of the boat while she sat in the very front to enjoy the breeze. Lindsey stayed behind because she had a terrible migraine, but likely she did not want to be around her. Lindsey was still angry she had left them.

Irene sat on Dawson's lap, and Emily smiled every time her daughter laughed. Dawson explained the lakes to everyone and pointed out the beautiful summer homes on the shores.

Once they reached Side Lake, he showed them his favorite restaurant, Bimbo's Octagon. "You should have dinner there before you leave. They make the best pizza around. Locals don't consider it a trip to Side Lake without Bimbo's pizza and wings.

Jamie wrinkled her nose at Dawson's comment. Emily moved to the back of the boat to talk to them while Dawson rounded up the skis.

"Bimbo's is a family restaurant, it's not like what it sounds. There are no strippers or anything. It was actually named after an old local guy who started the business. Bimbo was his first name."

Jamie laughed. "Oh good, I was a little worried about what we got ourselves into here."

"Can I sit up front with you, Auntie?" Josie said.

She was going to break this little girl's heart in a few hours. She would do everything she could to make her day before that happened." "Of course, but Dawson is getting the waterskies right now. Would you like to waterski first?"

Her eyes lit up. "I would love to. I go to Lake Mead and Lake Powell with my parents every summer and we waterski.

Well, we don't really waterski at Lake Powell, we usually rent a big house boat with a waterside and mom lets me bring a friend. We get our own room and when it's really hot we play cards under the boat. It's so cool. Have you ever been to Lake Powell before, Auntie?"

Emily was impressed. "No, I haven't but it sounds like a great time. Is it as beautiful as Minnesota?"

"It's almost like you're in the Grand Canyon. There are cliffs all around and they're so high. But here it's more exciting and fun. There's so much to see but in a different way. I can't compare the two. But the sun is not as strong here. Lake Powell is pretty much a lake surrounded by dessert. It's amazing."

"Here's the skis, who's going first?" Dawson said.

Josie jumped up and looked at Dawson with big eyes. "I am!"

"Okay, jump in and I'll throw them to you. I think I heard you're a pro at this, right?"

She giggled and jumped in the water. She screamed and her teeth chattered. "It's so cold!"

"Do you want to get out?"

She leaned back in the water and put the skis on. "No way. I'll get used to it."

Dawson pulled away slowly until she found the rope.

He stood up. "Ready?"

Josie nodded, and he guided Irene's hand on the throttle.

Emily held her long blonde hair back with her hand so she could watch.

Josie got right to her feet and her posture looked great. She had a slight lean and was going back and forth across the wake. Jamie held up her thumb and Josie did the same in return, with a smile. She went over the boat waves, jumping and getting some height. Then she performed a 360.

"Whoa!" Emily said. "That was amazing."

"They're trick skis, but she's definitely advanced for her age," Dawson said. He looked back and she did it again.

"How much time do they spend at Lake Mead?" He laughed. "I have my own boat, and I can't do that."

Irene went to the back of the boat and sat on her grandfather's lap. His eyebrow shot up and he grinned. He wrapped his arms around her and smiled.

After a long run, Josie dropped the rope and the boat circled around to pick her up.

"My arms are getting sore," she said.

"Where did you learn to do that? High five, girl," Dawson said. He extended his hand out to her in the water. "Emily's next."

She did not know how to ski. Sure, she went downhill skiing at Spirit Mountain with Gabby and at Giant's Ridge with Matthew. Was it the same thing? Well, she would soon find out.

She moved out of the way as Josie crawled up the ladder and dripped water on her toes.

"The water is so cold, Auntie. Don't think about it, just jump in."

"How am I going to follow up that performance? You're going to have to teach me all of your tricks."

"Adjust the skies with the lever on the side when you're putting them on. Once you get them on, Dawson will coax the rope to you. When he takes off fast lean back and keep your legs rigid."

"What if I fall?"

Josie shrugged. "Don't be frustrated if you don't get to your feet today, it takes time to learn."

Was she really only eleven years old? She spoke like an adult. Josie had her determination. If only she'd had the chance to know her as she grew up instead of living in fear all these years.

"Your turn, Em," Dawson said.

She stood on the edge of the boat, working up the courage to jump in. "I can't do it. It looks too cold. Someone else go. Jamie?

Jamie got up and pushed her off the boat. When she hit the water, she breathed in and choked on the water. She surfaced and coughed. "Why ... why did you do that?"

Jamie laughed. "You were being a baby!"

She tried on the skis. Josie had the same size feet as she did, which made it easier. She lay back in the water and held onto the rope until the triangle made its way to her.

"Ready?" Josie said.

"Ready as I'll ever be," she said.

Dawson took off and she squatted until her skis went in different directions and she dropped the rope. The boat came around and she did it again, falling sooner than the last time. Ten minutes later, she was ready to give up.

"Lean back farther this time and keep your legs and your skis straight. Let the boat pull you up, not your arms," Josie said.

At this point, Josie and Dawson were the only ones watching her. Everyone else had given up on her. But this time she would not fall.

Dawson punched the throttle and the rope tightened. She stood up, her knees bent. She was a little wobbly, but she did it. Everyone in the boat clapped except Dawson who was grinning. She focused on the middle of the boat stream where the water was quite dark. She thought about going to the side like Josie did but the wave she had to get over was too big.

A couple boats passed their boat and the waves got bigger. She let go in fear of losing a tooth or worse with an uncontrolled fall or being dragged across the lake on her stomach, an image she could not shake.

Josie leaned over the side of the boat. "You did it, Auntie. "Your forearms sore?"

"Horribly," she said.

She toweled off and sat in the front of the boat again. Dawson let Jamie drive and sat down next to her. Irene was sleeping in her grandfather's arms, and Josie was eating a sandwich.

The engine was loud and the wind strong. She rested her back against the boat and stretched out her legs to where the cushion v'd in the bow of the boat. Dawson did the same on the other side.

"Hey Dawson, I think we need gas," Jamie said.

He got up to put more gas in the boat and then he sat back down with her. He put his legs up and crossed his ankles. They were back on Big Sturgeon when Dawson released his ankles and touched her leg with his toe before getting up to take the driver's seat.

A current of electricity ran through her body at his touch. She couldn't stop thinking about the way he rubbed the cramp in her leg and helped her change. His bare chest resting against her back as he held her hands and taught her to use a pottery wheel. His tongue in her mouth, their amazing kiss. Why did she have to leave him that night? He probably thought she was a big baby.

By the time they reached the cabin, it was dinnertime. Everyone was exhausted except Irene because she slept for an hour on the boat.

While they prepared dinner, she rehearsed ways to talk to Josie and help her understand her secret, and why she kept it all these years. They had bonded on the boat. Josie looked up to her. She wanted desperately to tell her, but she was so scared. What would Josie say? Would she ever talk to her again?

CHAPTER 26

*N*o one talked much at dinner, they were all pretty exhausted from a day on the boat in the sun.

"Let's get your pajamas on, sweet girl," Emily said after Irene finished her dinner "We can read a book together. Your pick."

Irene wrinkled her nose. "I want Josie to read to me."

Emily glanced at Josie. She had a big smile.

Josie took Irene's hand. "Come on, I'll help you get your jammies on."

At eight o'clock they had dinner and visited. Even Lindsey came out to chat with them though she avoided talking to Emily.

But she was just glad Lindsey was there. They were never very close, not even when growing up. Their relationship became worse when she moved away. Lindsey felt abandoned, especially since she never answered any calls from her. But she could not listen to them talking about her mom's death, not talking about her mom at all. And then San Francisco happened, and she shut out her family because she was ashamed with what she did.

Growing up, she kept an eye on Lindsey when she was around Dawson, and then laughed for being jealous. That was years ago. Yet Lindsey still gazed at him with a yearning look on her face. She laughed at everything he did said while around him in the cabin, and she made a point of ignoring Emily. Lindsey was still the same clueless young woman.

IRENE FINALLY FELL asleep and she kissed her goodnight. She stopped outside Irene's door to breathe. This was it. Time for the secrets to come out. The moment she had dreaded ever since Jamie had announced they were coming to visit. Dawson had said anyone could crash at his house and that was good. Josie would likely never step inside her house again after she told her the truth.

She slipped outside and walked down to the dock with Jamie. They sat in silence for a while before Jamie said, "It's time, Emily. It's time to tell her the truth. It's time to clear our consciences, too."

She looked down at the clear water. She breathed in and out to calm down and gazed at the waves and the starry sky. During the day, the lake was so busy boating was dangerous, but at night after everyone had gone into their cabins the lake quieted. Some nights coyotes called to each other on the other side of the lake.

"I made myself believe it wasn't true, you know. I told myself if I stayed far enough away it wouldn't hurt so bad, but it did. I didn't even tell my husband or Josie's dad."

"She's going to ask who her father is, Em. I know her, and she's not going to let you get away without telling her."

"I can't. She's better off not knowing. He doesn't even know he has a child."

"She will never forgive you if you don't tell her. She's

eleven, she's going to want to meet him. Do you know where he's living now?"

Her stomach churned at the thought. "Dawson would know."

"What are you going to say? Do you want me to help?"

"I don't want this to fall on you. I'm going to tell her straight out. Josie, I'm your mother," she said, practicing her words aloud.

A gasp in the dark startled them. Josie stood at the end of the dock, a frightened deer in the headlights look in her eyes.

"Josie?"

Josie took off running. Emily jogged after her, but Josie was so fast she had a hard time catching up with her. Josie turned onto Greenrock Road, and she was catching up until Josie went over the bridge and headed for Sixberry's landing. She disappeared into the darkness.

She stopped running. Where did Josie go? She had to be hiding somewhere close.

HER WORLD FELL APART in 2009, and led her to this moment of having to face her biggest fear, of having to tell Josie she gave her up as a baby.

When she found out she was pregnant she called Jamie. "Can I come live with you?"

Of course Jamie said yes.

Once she arrived in San Francisco, Jamie and her boyfriend, Gregg, were so kind and generous. They went on walks, took the famous trolley, and visited Fishermen's Wharf docks to watch the seals. They even took a boat tour out to Alcatraz.

One sunny day Jamie took her to the Golden Gate Bridge so they could walk across it. The fog was thick and gloomy, and she was glad to be alone with her sister so they could talk about the future of her child.

"So what are you going to do?" Jamie said.

"I'm not sure. I can't raise a baby on my own right now. I had a pregnancy scare shorty after I moved to Minnesota with Jordan, and he flipped out. I just couldn't tell him that I was pregnant again. He would want me to get an abortion and I can't do that.

Jamie patted her back. "I understand."

"I feel so selfish, but I want to go back to school. I can't raise a baby on my own without a job or money, you know. I just don't know what to do."

"Why don't you stay here with Gregg and I, and we'll help you. We've been trying for two years to get pregnant, but I don't think it's in our cards. We would love to help you raise the baby."

"You guys have been so awesome. I've got to figure this out." She half-laughed. "I doubt you'd want me to live with you for the rest of my life. I can't afford to live here by myself, it's too expensive."

She thought about it every minute of every day. She needed to make a decision, but it was so hard. She considered an adoption agency, but put that idea to rest. Her sister and Gregg were so excited about helping her raise a baby, and that seemed like the only option she was okay with. They had the financial means. Could she live with the fact that someone else would be paying for everything for her and her child? They would have to support her until she got on her feet. The idea of being dependent on them was unthinkable.

She decided to swallow her pride and accept Jamie and Gregg's generous invitation to help her raise her child. They were so excited they started making a nursery. They were like the three musketeers. Gregg found a way to take time off from his marketing job to make all the doctor's appointments, and Jamie was a nurse practitioner at the clinic where they set her up with the best obstetrician around.

Her sister rubbed her feet and prepared the healthiest meals for her. They walked everywhere in San Francisco so she ended up in the best shape of her life. Every weekend they went to the farmers' market and bought fresh organic fruit and veggies.

San Francisco became her new home. She planned on returning to Florida at some point, but she made Gregg and Jamie swear not to tell Lindsey or her dad until she was ready. She was afraid something would happen, and she did not want any questions about who the father was. She told her dad she was on vacation in San Francisco, but not that she was actually living there.

Once she hit her eighth month, she was exhausted and in bed by seven o'clock every night. She couldn't stay asleep because her baby's kicking kept her up all night and she constantly had to pee. She wanted so badly to sleep on her stomach or back, but the doctor said she needed to sleep on her side.

June twenty-first, 2009 was a day she would never forget. She had a sore throat, stuffy nose, and a horrible cough. Then the diarrhea and puking started. She had a high fever fogged her mind.

When she started gasping for air, Jamie realized she needed to get to the ER. She couldn't reach Gregg so she left him a message and they took off. Once Jamie told the nurse of her symptoms, they took her into a white room with clear plastic all around it like a bubble. The nurses came back in hazard suits and the next thing she knew they were sticking a Q-tip so far up her nose she was pretty sure they were going to come out with part of her brain. They then stuck one in the back of her throat. By the time they returned, she was drifting in and out of consciousness. She remembered them saying she tested positive for H1N1, and they were extremely concerned about her baby. Her fever was 104 and would not break. Opening her eyes hurt so she could not do it for long.

Jamie and Gregg stood outside the isolation room wearing masks and scrubs, and holding hands and crying.

She fought to live, and to save her baby. The doctor put her on a ventilator, and the nurses described her as touch and go. One of the nurses said she needed to keep the baby inside her for a couple more weeks.

She would not give in and die. She kept fighting to live.

She was in quarantine for a week before she went into labor. The doctors tried everything to keep her from having the baby, but finally they recommended a c-section. Jamie was allowed in the delivery room. Gregg would follow the baby after delivery, and Jamie would stay with Emily.

She heard one of the doctors tell Jamie, "If you pray, do it now."

She was awake through the surgery. Josie's umbilical cord was wrapped around her neck.

The doctor lifted the baby up. "That was lucky. If we had opted for a natural birth, your baby would not have made it."

The baby was blue and quiet when they pulled her out. Emily could not stop shaking.

Jamie rubbed her swollen eyes. "What's the matter? Why isn't she crying?"

Josie finally cried after what felt like forever and that's when the tears began to flow in Jamie and Emily's eyes. Thinking back, that was when she felt the love Jamie had for her baby.

She recovered and was released from the hospital with baby Josephine. The fresh air outside the hospital felt so good in her weak lungs even though it made her cough. She stayed in bed for the next ten days, but she refused to let the swine flu beat her. Gregg and Jamie helped and she was finally able to sit in a rocking chair and hold her baby by herself for the first time.

She kissed her baby's face. "Oh sweet girl, I thought I was going to lose you there. We've been through so much together in your short time on earth, you know that?" She slipped her pointer finger inside Josephine's tiny little hand and watched her suck on the bottle.

She found her answers in Josie's sweet face, and she knew what she had to do, but it was going to be the hardest decision she ever made. "I'm not ready to be a mama," she said, wiping her tears. "But you're going to have two amazing parents. Don't ever think I didn't love you, okay? I need to do what is best for you and that means giving you away to two amazing people who will take good care of you. I'm so sorry, sweet girl." She kissed her forehead, removed the bottle, and put her in the basinet. She looked back at her, fast asleep already. The pain in her heart brought her to her knees. She bent over and covered her eyes as she cried. She had no choice. She had to do what was best for her baby girl, even if it felt like a part of her heart was being ripped from her chest.

Gregg and Jamie were ecstatic at the news and asked her over and over again if she was sure.

"I have one request and it's non-negotiable. You can't tell anyone," she said. "You can never tell anyone I'm Josephine's biological mother. Promise me you will forever keep my secret."

Jamie took her hands. "We understand, and we'll respect your decision and love her like our own."

"One other thing. I don't think I can handle being a part

of her life and watching her grow without it killing me. I need some distance."

Jamie nodded. "I hate that you won't be able to be around, but I'll send you a picture if that's okay. If you ever change your mind and want to be a part of her life, whatever that may look like, we will support any decision you make."

CHAPTER 27

"I don't know what to do. Should we call the cops?" Emily said.

Jamie cupped her hands and called out. "Josie! Josephine please talk to us, we're worried about you. Where are you?"

Jamie went one way and she walked back to the cabin, deep in thought. Where would she go if she were to run away? An idea struck her.

She ran back to Greenrock Road, across the bridge, and down the hill to the channel. Huge rocks were piled up under the bridge. She made out the dark outline of what looked like a person sitting on one of the rocks.

"Josie?" she whispered.

"I don't want to talk to you."

"Josie, I'm so sorry."

"I hate you, you aren't my mom. Why would you say that?"

She did not blame Josie for feeling that way. She had lied to everyone for twelve years. Jamie was right, she should have told her a long time ago.

"Will you come out and talk to me? Your mom is worried sick about you."

"I don't even know who my mother is anymore." Her voice cracked. "How could you just give me away? Are you really my mother?"

She walked across the rocks. "I didn't want to, trust me."

"Don't come any closer, you're a liar! I always wondered why I didn't have brown hair like my mom and dad. My whole life was a lie.

Josie was hugging her knees to her chest. A sad, little girl.

She did not know how to talk to her, how to explain. She was at a loss for words.

"Why didn't you love me?"

She sat down on the rock next to Josie. She expected her to get up and run away, but she only inched to the other side of the rock.

"I did love you, I do love you. It was the hardest decision I ever had to make."

She stared at Emily. "Then why did you give me away?"

Jamie came running across the bridge and Emily yelled out to her. "I found her, we're on the rocks under the bridge."

"I don't want to see her," Josie said, her voice deep and full of anger. "She lied to me."

"I made her promise not to tell you. I wanted you to have a normal life," Emily said.

"And look at what that did for you."

Jamie was standing on the opposite side of the channel. "Oh Josie, I was so worried about you."

"You don't care about me! You are a liar! I hate you!"

"It's not your mom's fault," Emily said. "I made her keep it a secret. I wanted you to have a normal life. I was young and poor, and I had no way to raise you on my own. I took the only sensible way."

"Normal? You call my whole life being a lie normal? You

left me as a baby and never even came to see me. Why? Was I that unlovable?"

She tried to hold back the tears, but Josie's words were ripping her heart apart. She thought she was being selfless, she thought she would never find out, but she could not tell Josie that.

"I was young and stupid. I thought it would be too hard to see you. Looking back now, I realize that was probably selfish. Your mom and dad tried so hard to have a baby and the moment you were born, your mom's face lit up. I almost died when I was pregnant with you and your mother took care of me, supported me. That was when I realized you would be better off without me. They could care for you in a way I couldn't have at that time. I loved you so much. It killed me to walk away and there hasn't been a day since that I haven't thought about you."

"Oh, lucky me. Did you ever think about how that would make me feel?"

"Of course I have, that's why I wanted to keep it a secret. I thought you would be happier if you didn't know."

"I'm eleven years old. Were you ever going to tell me?"

Josie's voice rang with bitterness. Couldn't she see this was what she wanted to avoid?

Josie was quiet and Emily waited for her to speak. "Who's my dad?"

Jamie spoke up before she could. "He was a boyfriend of your aunt's, and he wasn't very good to her. His name is Jordan. He's a cousin of Dawson's.

"Can I meet him?" she said.

She wanted to say yes, but she did not want to keep lying to her. Before she had a chance to tell her the truth, Jamie said, "Yes, we can find him if you want to, right Emily?"

Emily nodded and followed Josie up the hill to the bridge where they met Jamie.

"You owe me that," Josie said.

Jamie put her arm around Josie's back, but Josie pushed her away.

Josie walked a few steps ahead of them, not saying a word all the way until they got back to the cabin. She headed for her room and locked the door.

"She'll be okay, she just needs to cool down. I'm going to call Gregg. He can always calm Josie down," Jamie said.

Dawson was asleep on her couch with the remote still in his hand. She tapped him, and he jolted up, knocking his head against her head. "Ow!"

They both held their heads.

"I'm so sorry, Emily. Are you okay? You startled me."

"I'm okay." Now came the hard part. She waved for him to follow her to the dock. "Thank you so much for taking my family out on the boat today."

"It was my pleasure. I'm the lucky one. I'm really sorry about the head butt. Are you sure you're okay?"

She nodded and forced a smile. He was going to hate her in seconds. "I can't believe how many times you've saved my life over the years. I want you to know how grateful I am."

He sat down on the dock. "Is everything okay with you?" He tilted his head. "You're worrying me."

She sat down on the dock and patted the spot next to her. "Please sit down with me, I have something to tell you."

"Okay," he said and followed her instructions.

"Remember when I left Jordan for good and never said goodbye to you all those years ago?"

He moved closer to her. "Yeah. I don't blame you for that."

"I never told you why I ran. I was pregnant."

His brows shot up. "Pregnant?"

She turned away from his probing eyes. "I thought Jordan was the baby's father because we didn't use protection, but then when I found out my due date I realized that wasn't possible."

"What do you mean? It isn't ..."

"Dawson, Josie is your daughter. And mine."

He was still, not moving a muscle.

It felt so good to finally let that out. "Please don't hate me. No one knows she's yours. I was going to have an abortion and then my sister and her husband were so excited that I thought I could raise her with their help, but then—"

"Wait a minute. Josie, like Jamie's daughter Josie?"

She nodded, trying and failing to read him.

"She's my ...I'm a dad?"

"Yes." Her stomach was in knots. She held her breath, waiting for him to react. He was definitely in shock, and she did not blame him. She could not imagine being him and hearing this all these years later.

"And you didn't tell me? Why didn't you tell me?"

He jumped to his feet and paced the dock. His voice was angry, demanding. "How could you do this to me?"

"I was scared. I'm so sorry."

"You're sorry? You let me go on about the baby I lost and how I'd never be a father and the whole time this was just a game to you? Why do the dads get the short end of the stick? It was my right to know."

"I know, I'm sorry, I was scared."

"You're sorry? I have an eleven-year-old daughter and you knew and never told me? I was so depressed, you have no idea and then to hear this. What about me and my rights? You took that all away from me when you gave up our child without consulting me first. How could you be so selfish?"

She tried to reach out and touch him, but he took a step back and fell right off the dock and into the water. She got down on her knees to see if he was okay under the water. He jumped up.

"Are you okay, Dawson? I'm so sorry, I never meant to hurt you. Let me grab you a towel," she said. She was not sure what to do or how to make this right. He was hurting right now, and she was the reason for his pain.

"I don't want a damn towel. Does Josie know who I am?"

She shook her head. She should have told her, but she wanted to tell Dawson first. Jamie bought her some time because she thought Jordan was the father. She let Jamie think that in the beginning because she felt less guilty giving Josie up. If Jamie had known Dawson was the father she would have made her tell him. But Dawson had moved on, and she never wanted to see him again. She blamed him for finding someone else and leaving her. She was never good enough for him. He was with her sister and then the random chick at the party after they slept together. If he loved her he would have fought for her, and he would be fighting for her now.

This time she was letting him go for good. She had told him and now it was time to move on.

Dawson headed up the hill, stomping and groaning the whole way. He turned right instead of left once he reached her cabin. Was he going to tell Josie? She would not let him.

She ran up the hill. "Dawson, no!"

Josie and Jamie must not find out he was the father. How dare he tell Josie without her permission? Josie would be even angrier for being misled. She could not handle giving her more bad news. She was going to tell her, she just needed more time.

By the time she got up to the cabin, her father was leaning over the railing. He had that disappointed look she remembered so well. "I heard what happened, Jamie told me."

"I need to get in there to talk to Dawson before he tells her," she said, her voice shaky.

He blocked the door. "Slow down, what are you talking about?"

She had no time to explain. Why wouldn't he let her into her own house? She did not have any time to explain it to him. "Please, dad."

He stared at her with a confused look on his face.

She screamed in frustration. "Dawson and I are Josie's biological parents. There are you happy? Now let me in!"

He moved out of the way and she charged in, on a mission to stop Dawson if she wasn't already too late. She stopped when she saw them hugging in the hallway. They both shot her an evil look.

"Dawson's my dad and you didn't tell me?"

"I'm so sorry," Emily said.

"Sorry? Sorry? I asked you straight out and you lied," Josie said.

Jamie was behind them, shaking her head at her.

She turned around and walked out the door. She got in Dawson's boat without anyone seeing her and lay down on the floor. She had no excuses, and she could not win. She cried herself to sleep.

BRIGHT SUNSHINE BLINDED HER EYES, and birds chirping broke the quiet. She stumbled to her cabin and opened the door. The bedroom doors were open and no one was in them except Irene, who was fast asleep, still covered up in her bed just the way Emily left her the night before. She was thankful the chaos did not wake her. Lindsey was asleep on her couch, but everyone else was gone.

She took a hot shower to wake up. Her lower back was hurting from the floor on the boat, and she had mosquito bites on her arms and legs, even one on her cheek. They ate her alive, but she never woke up.

She went to check on Irene again, but she was gone. She called out for her and ran into Dawson in the kitchen.

"Irene and Lindsey are at my house right now. Everyone stayed there last night in case you were wondering."

She made sure her towel was tucked in tight so it wouldn't fall down. "I'm sorry, Dawson."

"I saw you get in my boat, but I didn't expect you to sleep in there all night."

"Please tell me how Josie is doing."

"She's a really great kid, you know that? She's doing pretty well under the circumstances. She's angry. She just found out she has been lied to by the people she loves the most in her life. How could you make Jamie and her husband promise never to tell her? I never thought you would do something like that."

She shook her head. "I thought it would be better for everyone. So she could live a normal life."

His sharp eyes pierced her soul. "I'm so angry right now. You aren't the person I thought you were. Your family is leaving tonight. They're planning on stopping by after breakfast to see you. I want you to know I'm in shock right now, and I don't know if I will ever be able to look at you the same way again."

"I'm sorry, Dawson."

His jaw set in a firm line. "What you did is unforgivable. I think it best if you don't contact me for a while, okay? Just leave me alone. I need some time to think."

He turned around and opened the door.

"No, Dawson, please don't go. I'm so sorry! I love you, I've always loved you."

He looked back and she held her breath. Would he ever be able to forgive her for what she did?

"You don't love anybody but yourself." And then he was gone

*a*n hour later Lindsey and her father walked in the cabin. Josie, Jamie, and Irene followed close behind.

Irene gave them a hug and ran into her room to play.

She gulped. "Hello," she said in a whisper.

Her father gave her a hug, but Lindsey walked right past her and sat down on the couch. Jamie stepped in front of Josie.

"Dawson is going to give us a ride to the airport. We changed our flight to fly out of Hibbing."

She looked out the window. Dawson was putting a duffel bag into his car, along with their suitcases.

"Well, that's nice of him," was all she could say. She felt Josie's eyes on her.

"We're driving their rental to the airport in Minneapolis," Dad said.

Emily took a step forward to initiate a hug with Josie but Josie walked out the door. Jamie gave her a half smile and a shrug.

"I love you," Emily said under her breath as they walked

away. It was almost as if Josie heard her and turned back, her eyes emotionless.

Dawson backed out of the driveway. He never even glanced in her direction. They drove away and disappeared when they turned onto Greenrock Road, but she kept staring down the street long after their car was gone. Tears threatened to overflow her eyes, but she could not move her arms to wipe them away. How had she screwed up so badly?

"You did this to yourself," Lindsey said from the couch.

"Lindsey, that's enough," her father said.

"No, dad, she's right. What I did was unforgivable," Emily said with her head down.

Lindsey stood up. "Oh, poor you. I don't think it's unforgivable, but I think you could have fixed things a long time ago."

She grabbed a Kleenex off the end table. "There's nothing I can do now."

Lindsey let out a loud, fake laugh. "Yeah, there is. You can fight for your family. All Josie wants is for you to love her. Don't you see that or do you just not care enough?"

Why was Lindsey so harsh? "What are you talking about? What is it you think I can do?"

Lindsey moved closer. "You always run, and you can't communicate for crap. You and Dawson were meant to be, even growing up, everyone could see it. The fact that you had his baby isn't a surprise. The fact that you had the baby but you did not tell him, I don't understand. He had a right to know. It's not just a random guy, it's Dawson."

"What do you know? That day at the beach, when I was too burnt to build sand castles with you guys, you were all over each other. I couldn't believe you chased Dawson in your skimpy little bikini. You two hid it from me for months."

Lindsey laughed even harder. "Dawson is hot, yes. I was young and chased him around because he jumped on my castle. But he loved you."

She sniffed. "That's not how I saw it."

"When Jordan sat next to you, I saw the hurt in Dawson's eyes. When you left with Jordan, Dawson had to walk away. It killed him to see you with him. The reason you thought Dawson and I were together is because he hid in his house for weeks when he found out you were dating his cousin. He punched something an broke his hand. And you didn't even notice."

"He did?"

Lindsey's account made sense. She was so caught up in her jealousy and giving Dawson a taste of his own medicine, she never noticed how badly she hurt him.

"I went to his house three times to check on him, but his mom said he wouldn't talk to anyone. She was so worried about him. You broke his heart and it seems like it's a pattern with you."

She never gave Dawson a chance to talk to her. Every time he called after that day on the beach, she cut the call short or told him she was busy meeting up with Jordan. She never realized the pain he endured. When she moved across the country with Jordan, it must have killed Dawson.

"So yes, I made you think I was seeing him, but really I was at the beach with Hannah."

"I didn't know."

"Your stupid jealousy and social failure has ruined our relationship and yours with all the people around you. I get it, you found mom dead, but who held you when you were a puddle that couldn't get up off the ground? Who was always by your side? Open your eyes, he has always loved you, but you can't stop hurting him."

She never wanted to hurt Dawson. He kept trying so hard to be with her. The kiss, saving her life, he was always trying to help her, but she failed see it. She kept crossing paths with him for a reason, but still she ran away from him. And Lindsey, she was obviously hurt by her, too. "I'm so sorry, Lindsey. You're my sister. I hope you can forgive me. I was terrible for cutting you out of my life, can you forgive me."

Lindsey hesitated then smiled. She hugged Emily and squeezed her tight. She was surprised at first and then pulled Lindsey in closer.

"That's all I wanted to hear. I'm your sister, Em, sisters forgive," Lindsey said.

"Thank you for forgiving me for being a stubborn, judgmental sister, then."

Lindsey scrunched her mouth and tilted her head as if in deep thought. "You're welcome. We can all be stubborn and judgmental at times, you just more than most."

Emily hit her arm and laughed.

"Now do yourself a favor and fight for your happiness," she said.

Her father stood up and clapped. "It's about damn time," he said. "I love you girls."

She walked her father and sister to the rental and waved as they pulled away. She did not want them to go. She had wasted so many years avoiding them.

SHE WENT BACK INSIDE and opened Irene's door. She picked up the pink blanket Destiny crocheted for her when she was born and covered Irene up to her neck.

She sat on the couch and went through the pictures on her phone of the day they were skiing at the lake. The ones of her and Dawson swimming at the lake were in there, too. She checked out the window, but his car was not back. She cleaned her house to keep her mind busy, and when Irene woke they went to the dock for a swim. Still no sign of his return.

Her mind kept returning to Josie. She had wonderful parents and a great upbringing. But the look Josie shot her, a look of hate, haunted her. How was she going to fix it?

She held Irene on her hip in the water, bending her knees so the water was almost up to their shoulders. Irene dipped her head back in the water and giggled. Irene had been through so much. First, Matthew was high at her birthday party and arrested for selling drugs. At least Irene did not watch him get cuffed. Then her father was away in prison for months. Her parents were divorced, which would change her life forever. And now she had a sister, though she did not know it yet. But Irene was resilient. She just splashed in the water, laughing like she had no worries in the world. When she smiled, she smiled with her eyes and lit up Emily's heart. She would never experience the same joy with Josie as she did with Irene, but Josie had a great life in San Francisco. She was so talented, and she could sure waterski.

It rained for the next two days so she and Irene spent the days snacking on ice cream and Doritos and watching Barbie movies. *Barbie of Swan Lake* was Irene's favorite. She checked for Dawson's car ten times a day. On the third day, the rain was still coming down and the temperature was chilly. She headed to the kitchen for a cup of coffee as a car pulled into the driveway.

She could not contain her excitement as she ran out the door in her bathrobe and bare feet. The scene from *The Note-book* and the sexy kiss in the rain between Noah and Allie, flashed through her mind. She wanted to hug him and never let him go. Apologize for all her mistakes so she could make them right.

The unfamiliar man stepping out of the truck stopped her in her tracks and reality hit. Dawson was not coming back. He was gone for good.

CHAPTER 29

The man had a confused look on his face as she ran up to him and then stopped abruptly when she realized it was not Dawson. The rain stopped almost as if on purpose so she could talk to the stranger.

The white truck had Kersich & Myer Carpentry on the side.]

"I'm Bill Myer," he said and held out his hand.

"Emily," she said. "Do you know where Dawson is?"

He shook his head, his smile friendly. "Sorry, dear, I'm just here to open up his house for the cleaner. He took a few weeks off, said something about a vacation or something. A cleaner is coming to get the house ready for a showing. He's putting it on the market. Too bad, it's a beautiful place. "

A dagger pierced her heart. "Why? Where is he moving to?"

"He didn't tell me. He's been acting weird. It's not like him to even take vacation, and he's not answering his phone now. Are the two of you close?"

How could she answer that question? They were very

226

close and now he hated her, and she was the reason he was leaving. "I guess."

"The real estate agency should be coming by later today to put a sign in the yard and take some pictures in case you see people coming and going. Anyway, I'd better open up the door. They'll be here in ten minutes to clean. Have a great day, miss."

She walked back into the house and called Gabby. "I know it is early, but I really need to talk to you."

Gabby laughed. "Me too. I have great news. Someone cancelled at the Greysalan Ballroom for the beginning of December so we can have a Christmas fundraiser this year! It's going to be a hit. Christmas at the Greysalon Ballroom, I have so many ideas. What do you think?"

The fundraiser was booked for this summer but after Matthew went to jail she told Gabby she could not do it. Gabby would not do it without her and insisted on moving the date back. They were hoping November or December, but the ballroom was booked.

She tried to work up some enthusiasm but failed. "That's good news, Gabby."

"What's wrong? Did you change your mind? Is it because you lost your job? You know, you could start your own business. I was thinking and—"

"No, it's not that. Gabby, I've lost everything and everyone. I need to see you."

"Then grab Irene and get your butt here."

"It's Matthew's week with Irene, but I'll come as soon as I drop her off."

"You better hurry. The suspense is killing me."

MATTHEW OPENED the door and smiled at them. He laughed and hugged Irene.

He had a little more shape to his face, and he was getting more muscular, which meant he was taking care of himself. "We came a little early, I hope that's okay."

"Better than okay. Jillian and I are planning on a day at Carey Lake, fishing and swimming with Irene."

Irene headed upstairs with Jillian to pack her bag for the beach. She was like a fish and wanted to spend all day every day swimming now. This move to the lake had been so good for them.

"You look really good, Matthew," she said.

He stepped aside. "Want to come in?"

"Just for a second. I'm on my way to see Gabby and Travis and the kids in Duluth."

"So weird, we're divorced, and my sister is closer to you than me. Then again, you're the sister she always wished she had."

She laughed and pushed his shoulder playfully.

"Seriously, I remember the first time my mom met you. She said she felt a strong connection to you. You were a piece missing in all of our lives until I started using again."

She felt the same way about his family. When his mom died she was a mess. Destiny was the glue that not only held the family together, but held her together, too. The one thing that helped her was knowing Destiny was reunited with her husband again after all these years. Although she never met their father, she felt as if she knew him from all the stories Destiny told her.

"What happened to your mom was so hard for all of us, but it hit you in a different way. You relapsed to numb the pain, but look at you now. Your mom would be so proud of you. You are stronger than your addiction."

He beamed. "I got a job."

"Congratulations, what are you doing?"

"Construction. I love it and I'm actually really good at it, too. Dawson offered me a job. Can you believe it? He's not so bad after all, even if he is dating my ex-wife. That's going to take me a while to adjust to by the way."

"Dawson?" Had she heard him right? "He offered you a job? When?"

"Like the day after I threatened him. He showed up and we had a good talk and we're cool. It's weird though, he was only at the site one day and then he went on vacation or something."

"Did he say where he was going?"

"No. Is everything ok?"

"Yeah, fine. If you do hear from him will you let me know?"

"No problem," he said. "Is everything okay?"

She squinted at him and nodded her head. "Are you sure you're okay with me, you know, moving on?"

"I'm happy for you, Emily, really. I mean it hurts to know Dawson will be a stand-in dad to Irene, but you know it was going to happen eventually.

She gave him a hug and called out to Irene, "Have fun."

"Bye, mommy."

"Matthew, I do need to tell you something. Will you walk me out?

He followed her to her car. The sun was shining a blanket of heat over the city and drying up any sign of the rain.

"Irene has a sister. When I was young, I got pregnant with Dawson. I was seeing Jordan at the time, and I decided to give my baby up for adoption without informing Dawson."

"Ouch. Does Dawson know?"

"Yes, I told him, and he just met his daughter."

"Does she live here?"

"No, it's Josie."

Matthew stared at her. "When I came back to the house

after, you know, I was gone. I found a box with hair and a picture. Was that Josie?"

"Yes, will you get it for me? I can't believe you found the box. I thought I lost it."

He hustled into the house and brought out the box.

She opened it and smiled, touching the lock of hair she hid in the back of her closet years ago.

"I'm really sad you didn't think you could tell me."

Emily frowned. "I didn't tell anyone. Not even Gabby."

"But I was your husband. You need to be more open with whomever you end up with. Whether it's Dawson or not. Learn to trust, Em. I know I didn't make that easy for you, but you need to or your relationships will never work."

What he said was true. She felt closer to him now than she ever did.

"What happened to your mother is not your fault. Let it go." He handed her a letter he had been holding. "This came in the mail. Josie?"

She looked at the return address, San Francisco, CA.

Once again he was right. She really liked this new improved Matthew. She kissed his cheek and pulled away. They were at the beginning of a beautiful friendship. That she was sure of. She would always worry about him, he was Irene's father, but she was not responsible for him anymore. He could finally be independent.

CHAPTER 30

*T*he letter bugged her the whole drive to Duluth. What could it say? Was it from Josie?

She pulled into Gabby's driveway. Gabby was waiting at the door. "Whoa, from the look on your face, this is serious. Grab a chair, girl and I'll pour us some wine."

She curled up on Gabby's overstuffed leather couch.

Gabby handed her a glass of Chardonnay. "Okay, what's up?" she said as soon as they were settled on the couch.

By the time she was done speaking, Gabby's mouth had dropped open. "Girl, you have too many secrets. How do you feel now that it is finally out?"

"I hurt a lot of people, but in a way a weight was lifted off my chest when it all came out. No more secrets, nothing to hide. Now, all I need to do is figure out a way to fix up the mess I've created from keeping secrets for so many years."

"How do you feel right now?" Gabby said.

Emily smiled. "I can breathe again."

Gabby patted her hand. "So, what are you going to do?"

"I have to find Dawson, but I don't know where he is. If he's not at the lake or working, where is he?" She shrugged.

231

"No one knows where he is. Sure his partner could be covering for him, but not Matthew. He would not lie to me, not after everything we've been through together." Dawson was gone and maybe forever. But she still had a chance to save her relationship with Josie. She had to try.

She pulled out the letter. "I got this letter mailed to Matthew's house from San Francisco. I'm not sure if it is from Josie or my sister."

Gabby changed position on the couch and bounced a little. "What are you waiting for, girl.? Open it."

Emily slowly ripped open the envelope. A folded piece of paper fell out. She opened it and looked at the bottom and saw Jamie's signature, not Josie's. Josie did not want anything to do with her. She dropped the letter into her lap.

"What are you doing? Read it," Gabby said.

"I can't."

Gabby reached over and snatched the letter off her lap. "Well, I can."

She did not try to stop her. She would rather read the emotion from Gabby than read it with her own eyes. The letter was short, just a paragraph long.

Gabby looked at her and then cleared her throat. "Hi Emily. I am sending this letter because Josephine, like you, is too stubborn to tell you the way she feels. She wants to be a part of your life, but she doesn't know how. Dawson has been here in San Francisco with us since we left. Josie wanted to go back with him to Side Lake for a couple weeks, and I know with a little push you could reconnect with her. They are flying out in three days. As her mother, I know her best and what I know is she loves you. From here it is up to you. I wanted to call you, but I didn't want Josie to know I contacted you. Please keep this between us. I was so jealous at first because I'm her mother and how do I compete with her biological mother? She is just so much like you. But I've realized this isn't a competition and there is enough of Josephine for all of us to love. Take care of our girl. Talk soon. Jamie."

Gabby stopped reading and wiped underneath her eyes. "This is your chance." She stood up and read the date at the top of the letter. "That's tomorrow. They are coming back tomorrow."

"So are you leaving me already?"

"Are you kidding? I'd make myself mad worrying about it. I'm spending the day with my bestie and her family."

"Great, let's get the pack together and head down to Canal Park. Travis will be so excited."

THE PARK WAS NOT AS PACKED as she expected it to be for a nice day. The pigeons flew overhead and strong waves coming off Lake Superior crashed into the huge boulders.

Gabby and Travis held hands in front of Emily. Melanie and Ben led the way and fought over whose turn it was to push baby Tia in the stroller. The kids stopped to sit on the huge three-foot boulders on the shoreline.

Memories of the day she fell and hurt her leg on the rocks when she was with Jordan came back. Jordan was a big part of her life then, but their relationship was toxic and she was so glad she got out.

Her past was her past, but if only she had told Dawson how she felt that day at the beach before she met Jordan. If she never met Jordan, she would not have moved to Duluth, and then she would not have found herself and had Irene.

Josie. Memories flooded over her, about having H1N1, about the c-section, and the way her sister and brother-in-law fell in love with Josie just like she did. At the time, she thought she was being selfless giving her baby away to someone she loved. If she could go back in time would she change that? No, but she would not hide that it happened. Hiding the baby from Dawson was not fair, but she was young and scared. That was what she needed to apologize for. Josie needed to understand she did what she did out of love.

Would Dawson have taken responsibility if she had told him? Would he have dumped Bobby and married her instead? That would have saved Dawson a lot of pain when he lost his wife and baby, but everything happened for a reason. Dawson was who he was because of the grief he survived. No, she could not rewrite the past, but she could make the present right. She needed Josie in her life like she needed air to breathe, and Irene needed to know her sister. She had no idea how their strange family would look. That was up to Josie. Whatever Josie wanted was what she would have to accept. Her heart was broken, but she was ready to put herself out there for her daughter. Finally.

GABBY SAT on a rock and Travis leaned over and kissed her when he thought no one was looking. Gabby smiled and grabbed his face in her hands. They rested their foreheads together and she pulled him in for another kiss.

Gabby and Travis were the proof she needed to see there are happy, healthy marriages. At times they argued, and Travis was often stubborn and uptight about money, which annoyed Gabby who would donate all their money to charity if he let her. They were opposites, but they fit so well together.

Melanie ran up and sat on Gabby's lap, while Ben ran with the stroller. Travis had to chase after him to take it back. He scolded Ben about being careful with Tia.

This family never took each day for granted. Melanie and Ben had been through so much with their bio parents and then Melanie's cancer, but they had a lot of balance in their life. Gabby and Travis made the children their priority, but they also made time for their relationship and their own dreams by always supporting each other.

They stopped at a shop for ice cream near the lake and ate lunch at Grandma's Saloon & Grill in Canal Park. By seven she was so exhausted she decided to stay the night in Duluth and head back early the next morning.

She was unsure of how she was going to win her daughter's trust back, but she would find a way ... she had to.

CHAPTER 31

*E*mily made it back to Side Lake by eight in the morning. She turned off Greenrock Road and into her driveway, hoping his car would be there but no luck.

Three big trucks were parked on the street and a "for sale" sign was on the lawn. Her heart sank. Would he come back to his place with Josie or was he gone forever? Maybe they were avoiding her altogether. Where would he go? There was no more beautiful place than right where he was supposed to be.

She turned at the sound of voices. It was the second-grade teachers: Jan, Liz, Ellen and the principal, Mrs. Voughn were speed walking past her driveway.

Her blood boiled hot, which gave her the energy to catch them. "Excuse me."

They continued to walk so she screamed it louder, and they all stopped and turned toward her. They scowled at her for making them stop, but she was sure there was also a little fear in their eyes. "Mrs. Fredrickson," Mrs. Voughn said.

"Actually it's just Emily."

Mrs. Voughn exchanged glances with the other teachers.

"I wanted to let you guys know you are the biggest bullies I have ever met in my entire life. You did not welcome me when I came to the school. You were rude and tore me apart. Are you all that unhappy in your own lives that you need to make others feel so terrible? You should all be ashamed of yourselves. You're teachers for God's sake."

They stared at her with their mouths open, unsure of how to react. She did not care. She had held her tongue for too long. "You guys are the reason Hibbing is known for being cliquey and rude. If you guys are good friends, that's awesome, but stop flaunting that you're better than others, and would it kill you to be kind and quit trying to leave others out? I mean come on, how do you sleep at night?"

Mrs. Voughn lifted her chin. "This is uncalled for, and we don't need to listen to this."

They turned around to leave, but once she started talking they stopped to listen.

"Oh you aren't one to talk. You told me I wasn't as important as the teachers are. Ask any good teacher if they could survive without Pupil Support Assistants to help with the children who need extra help. What makes you think a person is defined by their job title or that a job has anything to do with their worth? You should be very ashamed of your behavior. I am a damn good PSA and if you can't see that, that's your problem." She stopped to catch her breath.

"Is that all?" Liz said. Her body was stiff and her shoulders almost touched her ears.

"No, one last thing. You're like the kid whisperer, Mrs. Eli, but you always need a pat on the back, which I don't understand. You're only as strong as your team so if you don't start teaching your assistants and showing them how to do their job then that reflects poorly on you. You're way too talented to be such a bitch." She waved her hand. "Okay, now you can go along and have a great day. I've had my say."

They ran off in the other direction, their voice loud and angry, but they did not yell back at her. Maybe they knew she was right. She felt a little bad until she turned around and heard the clapping. It was Dawson.

HER FACE GREW HOT. Of all the times for Dawson to come around. She must look like a jerk to him. "How long have you been standing there?"

"Since you caught them. Quite a show, Mrs. Fredrickson," he said, mimicking the principal's words.

Where was Josie? Was she in the house or by the water? Or did she even come?

"I'm sorry you heard that."

"Are you kidding me? That was long deserved. That's the Emily I know. You were honest, and you weren't passive aggressive like they were. You didn't run and hide, you faced the problem head on and stopped caring about what they thought. That takes guts."

"Thank you. I'm sorry, Dawson. I'm so sorry about what I did."

He adjusted his Twins hat on his head. A nervous habit he had since he was a child. "Why didn't you just tell me we had a child? Didn't you think I deserved to know? Sure you were young, but what about these last few months when we've been pretty much inseparable? I trusted you. I told you about my wife, my daughter."

Guilt and shame washed over her. "I don't know why. I'm sorry. I'm really sorry." Tears rolled down her cheeks and her body shook. She hid her face in her hands.

He walked closer and tucked her head into his chest, and wrapped his arm around her. "I hate to see you hurting, but I can't wrap my mind around it. I'm sorry you felt like you couldn't tell me. Please from now on, no more secrets."

"Promise," she whispered. "Can I ask you a question?"

He pulled away so he could see her face. "What is it?"

"Are you selling your house to get away from me?"

He laughed. "Maybe I wanted you to think that to hurt you at first, but no, I found another cabin down the road. It's still on Greenrock Road, but I need a fresh start. This was the home I shared with my wife, and she will always hold a place in my heart, but I need to move on, and I can't if I'm still living in our past."

"You have no idea how relieved I am to hear that. And Josie? Where's Josie?"

"I'm right here, mom," Josie said. She stood on the front porch and stared at her.

She could not believe her ears. She wiped away the tears. "Did you just call me mom?"

Josie nodded, her eyes glossy.

She ran to Josie and wrapped her arms around her and cradled her head. "I love you so much, sweet girl. I'm so sorry, and I promise to be honest with you from now on. I never wanted to hurt you. I just wanted you to be happy, and I knew I couldn't take care of you."

Josie interlocked their hands. "I know. I'm sorry too, I was just so mad. I felt like everyone had been lying to me my whole life."

She examined Josie's fingers closer. They were identical to hers.

Josie looked into her eyes. "Will you be my mom again? I don't mind having two moms and two dads. That just means more presents at Christmas."

She cried and laughed at the same time. "I'd love that." She hugged Josie again, not wanting to let go of her. "I'm so glad you don't hate me."

Josie leaned in out of Dawson's earshot. "I would never hate you, but I think you need to go kiss my dad now. He can't shut up about you. I think he's crazy for you."

Emily wiped her tears with the back of her hand and sniffled. She turned around and there stood the man who would be her partner for the rest of her life. She remembered him as a child and now this grown, gorgeous man with the curly dark hair and beautiful eyes.

They moved closer and he took her head between his hands. She wrapped her arms around his neck. Their lips met and magical sparks flew. It was the next first kiss of the rest of their lives together.

She looked back at a hooting and hollering Josie. "Get a room, kids!"

JOSIE WENT inside the cabin while Emily and Dawson walked down the driveway hand in hand.

"There is one question I have to ask. You said Jordan is in Florida. What is he doing there? You gave me a strange look when I asked you before."

He stopped and turned toward her. "After the two of you broke up he married Marley and they moved to Florida. He turned his life around, Emily. They have two kids. He's doing well."

"I'm so glad to hear that. I don't hate him, you know." This was the first time she did not feel sick at the thought of Jordan and what he did to her.

"I know. I told him about us," Dawson said.

She held her breath. "And ... what did he say?"

"He's happy for us. Like I said, he's grown up. He went through some hard times, but he wishes us the best."

Another miracle. Her move to Side Lake was the best decision she ever made. All the best things happened to her on Greenrock Road.

"There is something I want to show you," he said. She followed him down to her dock and into the boat that was now in the water. He turned the key and it fired up.

"You fixed it! I can't believe it. Jillian is going to be so happy."

"I had some help from a friend," Dawson said. "Mr. Rivers was here looking for you and he saw me struggling with the boat so he helped me and in return I listened to what he had to say. He wants you to come back. He says he's sorry, and his business is folding without you."

Emily stared out into the water as the wind blew her hair around.

"Well, are you going to take his offer?" Dawson said.

"Nah, but I'm definitely going to call him because I want to hear him beg."

His voice rose. "Aren't you sassy? Let's pull around and pick up Josie on our dock."

"I could get used to this," she said closing her eyes. When she opened them, Josie was waving her arms in the air and she jumped into the boat with them.

"So, what do you think about Dawson fixing your boat? Sweet, wasn't it?"

Emily touched her arm. "It was very sweet."

"You guys are going to live happily ever after now, aren't you?" Josie said.

Emily nodded. "My life is now complete."

She looked up at the sky. Northern Minnesota was so beautiful. Sure it was freezing cold in the winter, but she loved all the seasons. The trees turning colors in the fall, building a snowman and having a white Christmas in the winter. Most of all, she loved the summer in Side Lake. The boats, jet skis, kids tubing, water skiing, four wheeling on the trails. For the first time since she moved here, she no longer dreamed of living somewhere else.

SEPTEMBER

EPILOGUE

The skylight in their bedroom brought in the sun and woke him five minutes before his alarm was to go off. It gave him five minutes to stare at her beauty and be grateful she was finally his. Her arm rested above her head on the top of her pillow. Her long, blonde hair half hung off the bed. Her jaw was relaxed, and her lips were slightly parted. He caught a glimpse of her perfect teeth. He ran his fingertips down her prominent cheekbone.

Her eyes opened and she turned her head and smiled. "Today is the day."

She gave him a kiss and then jumped out of bed with so much energy. She shut off the alarm before it rang and put on her jeans and pink sweater.

Dawson put on his favorite black dress pants and white collared shirt with a pink and blue tie. Josie had given it to him for his birthday last month.

By the time he made it downstairs, Irene was already eating breakfast and his wife was making Irene's lunch. A week after she gave those teachers and the principal a piece of her mind, Mrs. Voughn called to apologize for being a jerk and told her she would be honored to work with her again. Liz and Jan were conspicuously absent so she had no idea about their feelings on her coming back to the school.

"Hi, Daddy," he heard from the Alexa.

"Hello, sweet Josie. Are you excited for your first day of sixth grade?"

"Are you kidding, Dad. This is San Francisco, and I go to a private school. It's awesome. Uniform and no chill in the air. I don't know how you guys do it without freezing to death."

"You better still be coming up for Thanksgiving," he said.

"I can thaw when I get back to San Fran," she said. "How are you guys liking the new house? I can't wait to see it."

"It's not as big as the other one, but it does have a sauna," Emily said.

"Hey there, sis how's the weather?" Jamie said.

Emily laughed. "Going to be sixty-five today. Maybe you guys should move here."

Jamie laughed. "Not going to happen. Say goodbye, Josie. It's time to catch the bus."

"We gotta go anyway," Emily said.

"Wait one sec. Irene, you're going to love pre-school. Remember to listen to the teachers and that your big sister loves you." Josie blew a kiss.

Irene ran to the screen and kissed Josie's face. "Love you, sissy!"

"Now go get dressed," Emily said to Irene.

THEY PULLED up at Lloyd's Daycare. Matthew got out of his car at the same time. They all walked Irene into the building.

Dawson was worried she would not want to go. She was used to Jillian watching her, but she loved kids so maybe she would not cry too hard. Emily was nervous, too. As soon as they got to her classroom, Emily bent down to give Irene a hug

"Bye," Irene said before running over to a little African-American girl with a purple Jo Jo bow in her hair.

"Well, I guess she's going to be okay," Matthew said. He patted Emily on the back.

Matthew shook Dawson's hand and Dawson walked him to his car to talk to him about what he needed to get done at the construction site that day.

EMILY WALKED in the front doors at Dylan Elementary with Dawson by her side. They were greeted by a big smile from Mrs. Voughn, which helped Emily relax a bit. "It's so great to have you back. Liz can't wait to have you back in her classroom with Anna again. Anna is in the cafeteria. If you need anything, you know where I'll be. Congrats on your wedding by the way. How was San Francisco? We're all dying to see pictures," she said. "A wedding on the golden gate bridge? Sounds so romantic."

Emily blinked and exchanged surprised glances with Dawson.

Liz, Ellen, and Jan came up to say hello and they both hugged her.

"It is so great to have you both back. Come to the teachers' lounge during lunch, everyone brought in a dish for a brunch since you did not have a reception. There will be gifts and cake after school."

They thanked her and Dawson headed to his room while Emily made her way to the cafeteria to see Anna for the first time in three months. She was sitting at the table with a tray of fruit and a cinnamon roll.

She sat down next to Anna and waited until Anna noticed her.

Anna looked up and screamed. She jumped into her arms. "Miss Emily!"

"How was your summer?" she said.

"Good. Your necklace?"

Anna pulled on Emily's heart necklace with a picture of her girls inside. A wedding gift from Dawson. On the back EK & DK was engraved.

She was so excited to be back to work even though she had the best summer of her life. She got to spend so much time with Dawson and the girls at the beach and then they moved into their new home just a few houses down. It was smaller but cozier. She loved it. It was a fresh start to their new life together.

Matthew moved into his family cabin, and he enjoyed working for Dawson. They even hung out and went fishing together. His woman friend, Becky, came boating with them even though Matthew was still waiting a year for an official relationship. He had grown up so much during the summer, and it was so good for Irene to see them all get along so well.

Josie spent the last month teaching her to waterski, and she could get a little air and jump a few waves now. Dawson liked to wakeboard and his back rolls were pretty impressive.

She had pretty much repaired all of her shattered relationships, and she was no longer letting people's opinions stop her from being who she was. She loved her new self and she loved being a PSA again. The schedule was perfect with her family and she loved that she got to work down the hall from her husband. She was not in his classroom anymore because Anna was in first grade, but she was okay with that.

Life was not perfect but she was happier than she had ever been.

Anna got ready to take a bite of her cinnamon roll. "You need to finish your fruit first, okay?" Emily said.

Anna kicked her in the ankle and rolled onto the floor, kicking and screaming. "I want my cinnamon roll!"

Every seat in the lunchroom was full and every child and adult stared at her as Anna made a scene. Anna was wailing and kids close by were covering their ears.

She kneeled down next to Anna and smiled to herself. She was so happy to be back to normal even if every day was not perfect.

Made in the USA
Monee, IL
22 October 2021